The First Day

The First Day

Phil Harrison

Houghton Mifflin Harcourt
Boston   New York
2017

First U.S. edition

Copyright © 2017 by Phil Harrison

For information about permission to reproduce selections from this book,
write to trade.permissions@hmhco.com or to Permissions,
Houghton Mifflin Harcourt Publishing Company, 3 Park Avenue,
19th Floor, New York, New York 10016.

First published in Great Britain in 2017 by Fleet, an imprint of Little, Brown.

www.hmhco.com

Library of Congress Cataloging-in-Publication Data is available.
ISBN 978-1-328-84966-3

Printed in the United States of America
DOC 10 9 8 7 6 5 4 3 2 1

I was born again: I was the owner of my own darkness
—PABLO NERUDA

A self is a form of freedom, not a sort of thing
—JOHN CAPUTO

Ne pas céder sur son désir
—JACQUES LACAN

I

What do you want?

The man shook his head, his grip still firmly on the boy's shirt. The boy looked to Orr, his eyes pleading. Orr smiled, reached out his hand, placed it on top of the man's. He stared at Orr, five seconds, ten, then shoved the boy hard against the wall and let go. Orr continued holding his hand. The boy moved to run off, but Orr raised his other arm into the air and the boy, perhaps in submission to Orr's authority or perhaps out of fear, stopped and stood still.

You have to start somewhere; apocryphal wouldn't get a look-in. Orr was one of those men around whom stories accumulated, stories rarely troubled by facts. Still, this one rings true. An interventionist with his interventionist God. Like father, like son. He reached out and took the boy's hand. And he stood there, holding their hands, and he closed his eyes, and he prayed. For love, for forgiveness, for the peace of God which passeth all understanding. Go, and sin no more, he surely didn't say.

You'd almost have wanted him to though, I think, if you were either of them, the man or the boy.

The week before he met her he had preached from the gospel of Mark. *For what shall it profit a man, if he shall gain the whole world, and lose his own soul? Or what shall a man give in exchange for his soul?*

Anna Stuart was twenty-six years old at the time. Samuel Orr was thirty-eight. Anna was a Beckett scholar. She taught at Queen's University, in an office perched above the red-brick show buildings. She lectured her groups of avid nihilists while looking at people scurrying far below, like insects. When she talked of Beckett's image, in *Godot*, of life as a woman standing astride a grave giving birth, her own legs would open, as though she herself were the woman. Her students watched her, humoured and titillated, as their lives were reduced to dust behind her back.

Samuel Orr was married, and had three children, all boys. The eldest, Philip, was twelve years old, the same age, his father pointed out, as Christ when he first preached in the temple. It had become an affectionate joke between them: Orr would ask what Philip had been up to that day, and Philip would answer, in mock affront, Wist ye not that I must be about my father's business? Orr was the pastor of a small mission hall in east Belfast, an indistinct pebbledashed building on a side street off the Beersbridge Road. It sat between an off-licence and a piece of wasteland, knee-high weeds and broken glass. Location as metaphor. A large text hung above the door, gold lettering on red-painted wood:

ACQUAINT NOW THYSELF WITH HIM AND BE AT PEACE. JOB 22:21

It was the sign under which they met. On a chilly early-autumn evening, light draining slowly from the sky, she stood across the street from the mission hall, taking a photograph. He stepped out of the door just as she clicked the shutter. It was a film camera, an old Holga, so she couldn't check if he'd ruined the shot or not. He spotted her immediately. He paused and, nonchalant, barely missing a beat, stepped into a pose. The cheek of it, the charm. She smiled. He shouted across to her.

Shall I go back inside?

You can stay where you are, she said, raising the camera again. She stood, waiting. He stood, waiting.

Any cha—

She clicked, laughing.

Is this your church? she asked, once he'd locked up and crossed the street.

No. I'm just the pastor. It's God's church.

She smiled.

You're a photographer?

She shook her head. A hobby, she said.

And do you just photograph places of worship?

Is there anything else? she asked him. His eyes lit up, she said later.

The heavens declare the glory of God; and the firmament sheweth his handywork.

She paused, I imagine, before replying. The earth makes a sound as of sighs.

She tried many times afterwards to name it, the way he looked at her, opened her up. The way a farmer looks at a field he's about to plough.

Are you saved? he asked her.

An old woman walked past them, hand in hand with a toddler. Alright, Samuel, the woman said.

He nodded. I am, Frances. Alright, wee man.

They walked on.

Are you? he asked again.

What is that unforgettable line? she said. If I do not love you I shall not love.

It couldn't have happened quite like this, of course. What kind of answer is that, anyway? And she wasn't saved. The blood of Christ was foreign to her. Not like Samuel Orr. And yet, and yet.

Orr stood in Cornmarket, a small circle at the centre of five of Belfast's main thoroughfares. The roads led in different directions, not only geographically but to different times, contrasting expectations. It was 2012, and a tentative peace was slowly beginning to transform the city. The area hived with goths and skateboarders, teenagers trying out identities off the peg, ready to run. Pick one road and the Victoria Square mall loomed large, a cathedral of money, with priests and prophetesses and all the incense and iconry your weak heart could handle; the glass-domed roof drawing the eye to where God used to live. Another route took you towards the sex shops and pound stores and cheap, Asian-made clothes. One direction pointed to the loyalist north, where commerce competed with the flag for men's affection, and peace walls – irony unintended – kept one out or in, depending on disposition. Belfast: a grubby Cubist maze, beautiful in the way a deformed child is beautiful to its parents.

Orr stood in Cornmarket, his voice raised above the distant traffic and chatter of passers-by. At his side a small group of compatriots, fellow sinners, gospel tracts in hand. It was a bright day, but Orr's breath was visible in the cool air. He rubbed his hands together as he spoke. His voice was loud but not belligerent: And there were certain Greeks among them that came up to worship at the feast: The same came therefore to Philip, which was of Bethsaida of Galilee, and desired him, saying, Sir, we would see Jesus. Philip cometh and telleth Andrew: and again Andrew and Philip tell Jesus. And Jesus answered them, saying, The hour is come, that the Son of man should be glorified. Verily, verily, I say unto you, Except a corn of wheat fall into the ground and die, it abideth alone: but if it die, it bringeth forth much fruit. He that loveth his life shall lose it; and he that hateth his life in this world shall keep it unto life eternal.

Orr was not the only preacher in Belfast. *If they should be written every one, I suppose that even the world itself could not contain the books that should be written. Amen.* But Orr stood out; maybe his youth, maybe the sharp eyes, the lilt, the soft gravel in his voice. He himself would have dismissed all these explanations. For him it was the suppression of these, the suppression even of his own words.

On the streets he spoke only the scripture, no commentary, no opinion, no interpretation. No pleading.

If any man serve me, let him follow me, Orr continued, Christ's words complicated by his own charm. Anna was walking through Cornmarket that afternoon. She said that she heard the voice before she saw him, that it was the voice that drew her before she even realised who it was. She stopped and watched him. She watched his hands move as though levering the words, pumping them up from a well. She watched the hint of a smile form on his mouth from time to time. A self-sufficient smile, she thought, not a smile to convince or enamour, just sheer delight in the phrases themselves as they fell out, rebounded around him. There was a hint of the hedonistic about it. Some of them sucked on God's words like they were cough drops, but for Orr they were wine and honey.

Jesus cried and said, He that believeth on me, believeth not on me, but on him that sent me. And he that seeth me seeth him that sent me. I am come a light into the world, that whosoever believeth on me should not abide in darkness. And if any man hear my words, and believe not, I judge him not: for I came not to judge the world, but to save the world.

He finished and stepped backward, almost tripping over a kid on a skateboard. He held his balance by grabbing on to the boy, who did likewise. They both laughed, still holding on to one another. Anna watched him as he pushed the kid away, his easy familiarity, his fearless preparedness to be in his own body, the sheer physical fact of him. *Das Ding*, wrote Rilke, for want of a better way of putting it. She walked over to him as his companions dispersed to hand out their tracts. He spotted her as she came towards him. He smiled.

Anna, he said.

Samuel.

What brings you here?

I was passing. And then I heard the voice of God.

Anna loved this. The ambiguity, the way she teased him. From the very beginning, he couldn't ever be certain when she was mocking and when in earnest. Sometimes she wondered if love, for him, was a form of holy obligation, a way of closing the gap between other people and himself. Her excess, her impossibility, that part he could never be sure of, could never manage, created the space into which to move, to love. What would happen if that gap closed, if he began to know her? Would they become one, or would love run out for lack of space? Is it the same thing?

The wind bloweth where it listeth, and thou hearest the sound thereof, but canst not tell whence it cometh, and whither it goeth: so is every one that is born of the Spirit.

Anna smiled. That's what I was going to say.

Being courted with scripture. A flirtation of the gospel. Anna had never experienced anything like it; the rhythms and patterns of the poetry pounded inside her.

Anna was an only child. Her father was English, and had moved to Belfast to teach – architecture – in the early eighties. He met her mother, also a teacher, though of young children, within a few months of arriving. They

married in 1983, only a year after they met. Anna's grand-
parents approved of the match, felt that their daughter was
taking a step up an imaginary social ladder. They were
mildly religious, but neither their daughter nor her new
English husband adhered to any beliefs; none, at any rate,
they would deem necessary to acknowledge or defend.

Anna grew up in an environment of relative safety,
in so far as anyone grew up those days in Northern
Ireland in safety. She was born in 1986, long after the
most horrific days: the no-warning bombs, the Shankill
butchers, the bar massacres. 1986 was the year of the last
mass demonstration in Belfast. Unionists took to the
streets in droves, decked in flags and bunting, fevered
with Britishness. Paisley rallied the crowd, words like
butter. A man who could shout while whispering. A
couple of hundred thousand stood listening, watching.
And they lapped it up, all of them, the paramilitaries and
the churchgoers, common ground. Around a flag and a
slogan. Ulster says no. They staged a strike a few months
later – a 'Day of Action'. Neither of Anna's parents took
part.

Anna had everything she needed, and more: foreign
holidays and school trips, the banal measures of middle-
class success. Without siblings she became solitary. Her
parents stayed together until she was eighteen. She
moved to Durham to study and received a phone call one
day from her mother to say that her father was moving
out. Anna could recall of this conversation only a clichéd
numbness. She was a virgin at the time, and whilst she
was hardly naïve, the destructive joy of sex remained an
abstraction. Like most teenagers, she neither loved her

parents nor hated them, and so her father's leaving did
not feel like a betrayal, no more than her own leaving
had been. Isn't all growing up a betrayal anyway, she
would later say.

How's Beckett? Orr asked her.

Still dead, she answered.

I looked him up, he said. He could write. It's almost
biblical.

He was a good Protestant, Anna said.

It's more than that, said Orr. It's knowledge. We are
dust. It's easy to say. But you feel Beckett knew it in his
bones.

You're a literary critic now?

Orr smiled. It's not that difficult.

Anna pushed him, laughing. It was such a tiny moment,
insignificant really. And yet, and yet. Kingdoms are won
and lost in moments. It was the way he looked around,
so imperceptible and so blunt. He wanted to make sure,
she realised, that no one had seen it. The touch. And
she realised that he had already thought of her naked,
imagined the taste of her skin under his tongue. Jesus.

Belfast is a city without roots. Roots are nourishing: they
drag sustenance out of the ground, suck up water from
dark subterranean pathways into the light. In Belfast,
everything moves in the opposite direction. Flags, history, tradition, they all take light from the world and
bury it. We know this, those of us blessed and cursed

to be born here, but we do not know that we know it. Listen to the way we talk: the soft rhythms breaking into moments of harshness that surprise even us. Ulster. The name itself punches at you. How could it not say no?

But what better place for love to take hold? Love: nothing more derivative and nothing more surprising. They met in a coffee shop, a small room with too many tables. They talked of Christ and Beckett and anything else into which they could channel their desire indirectly, any container to hold the immediacy of their longing without it spilling into view.

They began to see each other weekly. The first few times they met in the same place. There was a determination in Orr, an attempt to keep it in public, as though if it were visible it would be safe. But God knows we have whole cities inside us, places to hide secrets from ourselves. A month passed. Anna fell ill, and cancelled their meeting. Orr hung up, then called back immediately. He offered to pick up groceries, whatever she needed, and bring them to her. It was the first time he had been in her house. She lived alone in one of the tall terraces off the Lisburn Road, near the university. The rear windows looked out on a small garden, backed up against the rear gardens of the neighbouring street. A couple of old oak trees provided privacy and shade, and housed scores of birds in spring and summer. Anna would waken to a cacophony of birdsong. Between and beyond the trees were the harsh lines of the hospital buildings, and further still the dark mound of Black Mountain and Divis, hunched over the city like silent witnesses.

*

Bataille wrote: *Reproduction implies the existence of discontinuous beings . . . Each being is distinct from all others. His birth, his death, the events of his life may have an interest for others, but he alone is directly concerned in them. He is born alone. He dies alone. Between one being and another, there is a gulf, a discontinuity . . . But I cannot refer to this gulf which separates us without feeling that this is not the whole truth of the matter.*

We are made through an act of fusion, Bataille says, a brief moment of continuity between two lovers, and yet we are born into discontinuity, the inevitable trappedness of being only oneself. *He is born alone. He dies alone.* All our lives we long to return to that continuity from which we were made. But there is only one way to do this: to die. This is too much, of course, so we seek out in life moments of approximation, moments when we lose ourselves, when for brief seconds I no longer exist, being part of something, someone, beyond myself. The mystics, beholding in their starved asceticism the face of God, forgot themselves, cried like wolves or children, lost in awe. Lost, literally. Boundaries dissolved, no reflection, no mediation. They say some glowed so bright you couldn't look at them for fear of blindness. And the lover, bound together to the beloved, penetration eroding for the briefest of moments the lines between, the discontinuity. Can you imagine, never having seen humans before, stumbling upon a coupling? How could you describe such a creature?

Orr was suspicious of charismatics. For him, God was bound up in the word, in scripture. *So shall my word be that goeth forth out of my mouth: it shall not return unto me void, but it shall accomplish that which I please, and it shall prosper in the thing whereto I sent it.* The shakers,

the speakers in tongues, the layers-on of hands: Orr
kept them at a distance, even in his own imagination.
But they crowded inside him, refusing to be silent. He
wanted comfort, and to comfort others; but he did not
want a comfortable God.

It wasn't that he feared the voice. The scriptures could
not have been more loved by anyone. But the wind
bloweth where it listeth, and Orr was not so foolish
as to believe that he could control or pacify it. Words
were one thing, wind another. He loved the words as
he loved his children: inevitably, obviously, in blood.
But he desired God like a woman. Passion, surprise;
the unknown pathways of the heart. He knew that the
words held life, and hope. But there was something else,
something beyond. Orr wanted *continuity*.

And this, Anna said, was the attraction. He was hand-
some enough. He could stand upright in a room in a way
that drew from others both authority and warmth. A
not inconsiderable quality. He listened to you when you
talked. But it was his connectedness, his sense of being
caught up in the unfolding presence of God in the world,
that struck her as extraordinary. It wasn't that he was
constantly trying to make everything holy, but that, for
him, there was no line between the sacred and the pro-
fane. The categories were meaningless. Anna said once
that in the early days she could not shake a picture of
him as – blasphemy upon blasphemy – the young Krishna
being scolded by his foster-mother Yashoda and opening
his mouth to reveal the Seven Oceans, the vast expanse
of the entire universe in all its glory.

*

Those few weeks, as Anna recovered – she had a mild case of tonsillitis, but it took nearly a month to clear up – were, as she remembered them, stark and beautiful. She was weak, tired. Her vanity protested Orr's presence; she wanted him to see her healthy and alert. But Orr's attentiveness, his persistent humour, outpaced her reluctance. She found herself longing for his arrival; waking in the morning to realise he wouldn't be visiting, she felt the weight of the day descend on her, empty and monotonous. They talked, or rather he talked, her throat resisting. And somehow, incrementally, he touched her.

Incrementally. It was like evolution, she said. No sudden moment, no threshold crossed. Now fish, now primate, now human. No point at which one ended and the other began, and yet they were separate, discrete. Continuity and discontinuity. In the beginning, they did not touch. But now. His hand strokes her arm, pushes hair from her face. He kisses her cheek as he leaves, like a French film. She lies staring at the ceiling, his footsteps on the stairs, the door closing behind him, the engine of his car choking into life. She cannot think, her mind a mess of impressions, longing. *What is that unforgettable line? If I do not love you I shall not love.*

Looking back, it struck Anna that she had no memory of the first time they slept together. Or rather, no single memory. Everything became memory, her entire body, not just her mind, a container. He flooded her, she said.

II

Orr continued to preach, his fervour undimmed. Some later said they noticed a change, but you have to take such re-readings of history lightly; how tempting to mistake hindsight for wisdom. The year was rushing towards Christmas, as it does in Belfast. The days shorten, darkness takes over. The rain, a steady presence throughout the year, becomes colder, the angles harsher. But then those days come like an unexpected grace: green and yellow and brown leaves littering the pavement, the early dew glinting, flickering in the low sun. Orr took to walking by the Lagan, through cut glens where cows, motionless, chewed their slow way through winter. The banks of the river were sparse and dun, mute birds aware, taking flight as he passed, leaving thin twigs trembling. Sometimes he walked as far as Lambeg, past the old brewery, out into open fields. He went out to find God, he told his wife, to listen to the Spirit. Maybe he did. Or maybe he was trying to walk himself out of love.

At times he would visit Anna after these walks. His cheeks flushed pink, burrs on his trousers. His hands were freezing, and he put them between her legs to warm them up. Sometimes they just lay there, his hands against her, between her, naked and quiet. He looked at her like he was trying to find something, she said, and every time he left he seemed to have a satisfaction, like he had glimpsed what he was looking for. She felt both exhilarated and unnerved by it; the sense that it wasn't really her he was after, but something inside her. She asked him once what he was looking at. He was standing naked at her bedroom window, framed against a grey sky, like an art installation. He was watching her, saying nothing. She lay on the bed, propped up on an elbow. This nakedness a gift, something he gave her which everything that followed could never erase: the feeling of being at home in one's body. He looked at her for a long time before answering. And Moses said unto God, said Orr, Who am I, that I should go unto Pharaoh, and that I should bring forth the children of Israel out of Egypt?

So much of Orr remained impenetrable to Anna. She felt like Marlow, moving deeper and deeper towards Kurtz, staring at the passing riverbanks, still understanding nothing. But the river carried her, and the sense of discovery was palpable, invigorating. She was both hunter and hunted, the thrill of capture alternating with the fear of being captured. She had both too little of him and too much; even in his absence her body felt more alive, her awareness heightened.

•

The months that followed were joyous. Anna was visited by Orr as often as he could without raising suspicion. His church and home were in the east of the city, far from the student bars and upmarket boutiques of the Lisburn Road, where Anna lived. Belfast had been ripped apart, ghettoised by the Troubles. Interfaces, walls, twilight zones. Orr's area was dominated, more or less, by loyalists. The children of the 1986 generation of no-sayers, they were just as militant, though with less to lose. A decade of unimaginative leadership, of reconciliation attempts built around 'telling your story', served for the most part merely to trap people in the failed myths they'd grown up with rather than encouraging them to abandon them for bigger, messier ones. Belfast was left with the veneer of a cohesive city, but was deeply fractured below the surface. More 'peace walls' were built in the ten years following the IRA ceasefire in 1994 than in the previous twenty.

Still, Orr could travel to Anna's part of the city easily, and whilst they avoided venturing out in public, he wasn't in great fear of being discovered visiting her house. There was a routine to their time together. They almost always made love first, no small-talk or awkward uncertainty. After the first month, as their intimacy increasingly matched their desire, Anna would often answer the door naked. At times she would touch herself before he arrived, so that from the first second her nerves would pulse. After the sex were long hours of lying around, afternoons bleeding towards evening, spring revealing itself slowly outside her bedroom window. When Orr wasn't looking at her he often stood by the window, watching the world taking shape again, recomposing itself after the death of winter. She watched his concentration, followed the lines of his body.

They spoke of everything but their relationship, the two of them combined. Orr talked of God fearlessly, seemingly unconcerned that he was standing naked in front of a woman not his wife. It's hard to make sense of this. Orr loved God and his word. And he loved a woman in direct contradiction of this word, even a most liberal interpretation. Neither of these realities is necessarily surprising. Whilst Orr kept it a secret, there was a sense in which he wasn't hiding. As he stood naked before Anna, he also stood naked before God, and you'd have to think that he was as aware of His eyes as of hers. There was a boldness in Orr's love, or at least in the exercise of it. He was daring God to prove him wrong. To intervene. In the middle of a rare argument, Anna accused him of being a hypocrite. What would Jesus do? she asked him. Orr was halfway putting his clothes back on. He stopped, looked at her, and said: He would do this. And he removed his clothes again and moved his mouth between her legs and began to kiss her.

Blasphemy is so close to devotion. The believer knows God, knows him intimately, not through rules and laws and books but in his heart; he feels God move through his body. *The letter killeth, but the spirit giveth life.* Orr tied himself to this like an anchor. He did not try to justify himself, but called on God to prove that he would have done otherwise. He was not one of those men constantly second-guessing their infidelity, moving from lust to

regret within the hour. Orr committed to his desire, and
whatever selfishness that entailed, it was not the selfishness of dragging Anna into his own guilt.

And so it went. Three, four times a week he called on
her and they spent a morning, an afternoon together.
Only once did they break the routine. An elderly uncle
of Orr's died in Scotland. Orr could have sent his condol-
ences in a letter, but he decided to go. The funeral was
in Elgin, a small town just to the east of Inverness, once
a cathedral city. Orr's ancestors had strong ties to Moray
and Aberdeenshire. His father, although born in Belfast,
talked with just a hint of Scottish burr, inherited from his
own father, who had grown up in Aberdeen and moved
to Belfast in his twenties. As a child Orr spent three or
four summers in the hills and mountains of the region,
and would always talk warmly of the towns he then
visited: Lossiemouth, Buckie, Fraserburgh, Peterhead,
Macduff. They sounded, to his young ear, close enough
to be familiar but strange enough for the promise of
mystery. He told Anna that it was in Peterhead that he
got saved. His father took him to a tent mission in a field
beside a gospel hall. Orr was ten years old. The preacher
was a man named Lousse, white hair streaked with grey
and black, like an animal. He was stout, his belly roundly
pushing at the buttons of his shirt, his tie never settling,
flapping with the movement of his arms as he preached.
And his voice was like singing, Orr said, a rich, round
brogue that practically sucked you into the kingdom.
Orr had heard it all before: ye must be born again, suffer
the little children, come unto me all ye that labour and

are heavy laden. For God so loved the world, that he gave his only begotten Son, that whosoever believeth in him should not perish, but have everlasting life. It was not news, as such. There was a sense in which Orr, even at ten, already believed it; he just hadn't committed to it. But something was different that day as Lousse spoke, Orr said. It was a different text, a stranger text. Lousse preached from John 12: Except a corn of wheat fall into the ground and die, it abideth alone: but if it die, it bringeth forth much fruit. He that loveth his life shall lose it; and he that hateth his life in this world shall keep it unto life eternal. There was something in Orr that leapt when he heard those words. The attraction of hating one's life. God knows what battles we fight with ourselves. Ten years old. He committed himself to Christ that day, Orr said, Christ in his brokenness, Christ in his death. And I, if I be lifted up from the earth, will draw all men unto me.

So Orr went back, and brought Anna with him. Anna travelled on her own, rented a small cottage at the edge of the Cairngorms, and Orr stayed with her. He travelled in and out to Elgin, meeting family members, sharing his grief and consolation. He told people he was staying in a hotel, and more than once had to resist an offer of a spare room. He was very nearly caught out. On one occasion, a cousin called unannounced at the hotel he had named. Orr's name was nowhere in the register. The cousin asked him on the following day, and he had to quickly come up with an excuse, namely that he had moved somewhere closer to the mountains.

For the four days and nights of the trip, Orr and

Anna were as husband and wife, shut off from the world. Anna looked back often on this time with such fondness it was almost cruel: the unfilled outline of what might have been. For four days and four nights they drank tea, talked, sat in the shape of each other's bodies on a bench in front of the cottage watching the dusk descend and the mountains fold in on themselves, the colour fading slowly until all was darkness. They woke to the sound of their own breathing. Birds, different birds, sang outside their windows. Once Anna, standing at the window, spotted a deer move across the low slopes of the nearby mountain. It was maybe two hundred yards away, but it turned as though it realised it was being watched, and stared in her direction. Orr was lying in the bed. She opened her mouth to tell him and then stopped, decided to keep it to herself, this moment of grace, this recognition. She turned to look at him. When she looked back towards the mountain, the deer was gone.

Orr's uncle had been well known and well loved in the town, and Orr found himself surprised by the connection he began to feel. Every day Anna watched him drive off towards Elgin, thirty miles away. When he returned he would repeat the stories he had heard, stories of faith and humour and kindness, and occasional mishap. His uncle had died well into old age, but not all in the family had been so fortunate, and the recounting of lives cut short seemed to give him a sense of himself that swelled at the edges. He shared these stories with Anna as though they were gifts.

Anna spent the hours while he was away reading, and occasionally writing. At this stage in her life (still well shy of thirty) she had published only her PhD thesis, an examination of the influence of German romantic paint-ers on Beckett's later plays. Already there were signs of the writer she would become, her wit tied to stark, blunt expressions. She took those German words that sound too good to be translated – *Schadenfreude, Weltanschauung, Gemütlichkeit* – and built a style out of their geometry: precise, full in the mouth, melancholic.

Her first collection of poetry came a few years later, but some of the poems that appeared in it date from this time. Edited and honed for many months afterwards, but born of the curvature and scent of the Cairngorms. On the night before they left, Orr arrived back to find her hunched over the small wooden desk, writing by candlelight.

Show me what you're writing, he said. She wouldn't. He smiled. Are you writing me?

Would you like me to? she asked.

A disturbance into words, a pillow of old words, he said.

She stared at him in surprise. You're quoting Beckett now?

He laughed.

She knew then, she said later. Who could doubt her?

Two weeks after they returned from Scotland there was an accident in a small row of terraced houses near

Orr's church. An unattended gas fire exploded, ripping apart a living room. An elderly couple, asleep upstairs, just managed to escape. But the fire spread quickly, catching the neighbouring house and racing through the downstairs rooms at speed. The furniture was old and cheap, highly flammable. Upstairs there was a young woman and her baby, four months old. The fire trapped them at the top of the house and the woman yelled from the windows for help. Neighbours rushed into the street but the flames from the blaze kept them well back. In desperation, the woman threw her baby to a man standing as close as he dared. But her throw was poor and the child hit the ground heavy. When the woman realised what had happened she moved back from the window, and disappeared from view, into the blaze.

Orr presided over the shared funeral. The tragedy was front-page news, and hundreds came to pay respect. Somehow people identified with the woman, or perhaps the child; the overwhelming futility, the powerlessness. It did not require a revolutionary spirit to see the story as one of poverty: gas heaters, cheap furniture, houses rammed close together. Class was never a major rallying point in Belfast: too deep and well exploited were more colourful histories of belief and tradition. And yet, like everywhere else, the experiences of the poor moved quickly through history and religion towards the broader church of cheap food, reality television and unemployment. Anxiety was free currency in the city; unnamed resentments simmered, inarticulable. A blurred, passive violence combined with outrage. No one knew quite where to direct their anger, and yet anger seemed in endless supply.

It was in this setting that Orr had to put two bodies in the ground. Anna saw an intensity in him she had not witnessed before. He was quiet, focused, his sadness palpable but not indulgent. When he visited her he moved around her house as though it were a boxing ring.

At the funeral Orr spoke quietly and without sentimentality. The woman had no relatives present, and perhaps this gave him a freedom he would have found difficult to create under the expectations of family members, lovers. He praised the woman, and the child, and the neighbours. He said that platitudes had no place on a day like this. That if comfort were to be found, it should be found in each other, in the physical presence of the people you can reach out and hold, and love. He said, to an audible murmur, that God should be ashamed. And then he read Psalm 137: By the rivers of Babylon, there we sat down, yea, we wept, when we remembered Zion. We hanged our harps upon the willows in the midst thereof. For there they that carried us away captive required of us a song; and they that wasted us required of us mirth, saying, Sing us one of the songs of Zion. How shall we sing the Lord's song in a strange land? If I forget thee, O Jerusalem, let my right hand forget her cunning. If I do not remember thee, let my tongue cleave to the roof of my mouth; if I prefer not Jerusalem above my chief joy. Remember, O Lord, the children of Edom in the day of Jerusalem; who said, Raze it, raze it, even to the foundation thereof. O daughter of Babylon, who art to be destroyed; happy shall he be, that rewardeth thee as thou hast served us.

He omitted the final verse: *Happy shall he be, that taketh and dasheth thy little ones against the stones.*

Everything changes, but there is nothing new under the sun. As a child, without brothers or sisters, Anna had to constantly invent ways to amuse herself. She created a game in which she would hide items of her mother's – hairbrushes, necklaces, even shoes – around the house. At first it irritated her mother and she complained. But the hiding places were obvious, a cupboard she would open regularly, where the teabags were kept, or under her coat. Her mother warmed to it, began to appreciate these deliberate surprises, these tiny gifts. Anna did not forget, though she'd been only six or seven years old at the time, seeing her mother change her mind, moving from irritation to joy. And she was struck that the only change was inside her, that her mother was choosing something; that the world existed, in some measure at least, *within*. She was not, obviously, able to articulate this at the time. But it triggered in her, the memory of it, she said, a mute awareness, a responsiveness, a deter-mination to create the world as she walked through it. By appreciation, by openness. By grace.

The funeral did something to Orr. His faith up to this point was hardly naïve, but from this point it tight-ened, hardened. It became leaner. It did not dissipate, fall apart as one sees among liberals, disappointed by their God being less powerful, or less nice, than they think themselves, and therefore dismissible. Orr's faith was more biblical, more brutal. If God needed fought, Orr would fight him. There was a violence in Orr. He would not lie down and let God walk all over him. An arrogance, perhaps; but isn't all faith arrogance? A universe stretching out towards eternity in both directions, uncountable creatures scuttling over the face of the earth: yet God loves me. Why not, of course. If you're going to have a god, you may as well have a decent-sized god, and one that pays attention. Not, for Orr, a cringing deity, full of love for mankind but utterly unable to lift a finger to help. His God may indeed stretch out the heavens like a curtain; but his hands were dirty.

Orr carried this attack into the bedroom. Always attentive, he became, said Anna, more physical. He was everywhere.

She asked him if he thought God would punish him.

For what?

For this, she said. You and me.

Of course He will, he said.

He came to visit, a Tuesday afternoon. He followed her into the kitchen. She put water on to boil. He knew something was the matter. He waited for her to speak.

I'm pregnant.

He nodded. Okay.

She shook her head. Okay?

He looked at her.

What do you want to do? she asked him.

He walked over to her, standing by the stove, and put his hands on her belly. He was silent for a while, watching her belly, watching his hands.

We'll have a child, he said.

How can we have a child? Anna answered.

People have been doing it for decades, he said.

Anna was prepared for anger, or fear. Instead she experienced an unexpected calmness. Orr made cups of tea for them both and they sat at the small wooden table.

Will you tell your wife?

Orr nodded.

Will you leave her?

He looked at Anna.

Do you want me to leave her?

I love you, she said. If I do not love you I shall not love.

They did not say much else that day. A simple satisfaction settled in Anna, chasing away her expected anxiety. She wanted the child; it is not a complicated desire, she reckoned. The weight of the world lies behind it.

Everything changes, but there is nothing new under the sun. Orr told his wife. He made no excuses, no arguments. He told her as clearly as he could, he said, that he had met Anna and she had become pregnant. Sarah surely asked him for details and he surely provided them. Whether this was a kindness or not is hard to say. By Orr's account, Sarah was measured in her reaction. Her anger was real but not showy, as he had expected. She asked him what he intended now to do, and he told her that he didn't know.

*

Orr continued to see Anna, though after she announced that his child was growing inside her, their physical intimacy abated. They still had sex, but more gently, and less often. She did not know at the time whether this was a temporary or permanent change, but in the aftermath of such persistent physical pleasure, its absence felt like pain. With the rawness of intimacy tempered, there were small gaps opened up in their conversations, spaces of uncertainty which had once been filled by sex. Orr still looked at her with longing, with desire, and his hands still moved over her. After the initial conversation Anna did not press him on whether he would leave Sarah and his family; but his continued return to her house was an answer, or answer enough. His faith was not diminished, neither in God nor in himself. Anna recalled a particular conversation, a week after her announcement. She was lying on her sofa, Orr making tea. She mentioned an article in the newspaper she was reading, about global warming, the melting ice caps, oil running out. She wondered aloud about their child, what world she or he would grow up to inhabit. About how we need to learn to care properly for the earth. Orr appeared at the doorway, the kettle rumbling behind him.

All these people talk about how we need to do this for the earth, do that for the earth, he said. The earth doesn't care. It doesn't matter to it whether it's covered in ice or sand, ants or people. The planet feels nothing. It's all narcissism. Talking about what the planet needs when what they're talking about is themselves. How can the selfishness that created this mess get us out of it? Deep down people know this, somewhere inside them. That's why humanism and secularism can never save the day. We need God, someone to lift us outside our own vision, to let us see the planet as creation – as though it did feel something. Have ye not known? Have ye not heard? Hath it not been told you from the beginning? Have ye not understood from the foundations of the earth? It is he that sitteth upon the circle of the earth, and the inhabitants thereof are as grasshoppers; that stretcheth out the heavens as a curtain, and spreadeth them out as a tent to dwell in.

Anna watched him, bemused. A smile appeared on his mouth, and he moved out of his rant, shaking it off like wet clothes.

He moved back and forth, between his own house and Anna's. What was it like, returning home, putting the key in the lock of his front door? His heart speeding up, slowing down. Sarah, hearing him arrive, moving further into the house, retreating. The boys not understanding what was happening, but sensing invisible chasms open up between rooms as their parents moved around them.

Orr spoke so rarely of Sarah to me; but the few times he did it was of a woman whose kindnesses were relentless, who loved him and his boys with simple devotion. Anna was not a refuge from unhappiness, nor a reaction to a felt hurt. Orr said he did not stop loving Sarah, but rather – now I speculate – he felt his desire widen, expand. Her patience – was it patience? – as he hauled an affair before her, set it up and told her what it was but not what to do with it. What was she supposed to do with it?

*

Anna had few people she would have called friends. Her fellow lecturers were amiable, one or two genuinely enjoyed her company, but for the most part she treated them, and they her, with a professional courtesy and restraint. Outside of work she kept largely to herself; a yoga class a couple of times a week, a monthly film club at the university theatre, occasional nights out for drinks with colleagues. She still saw her mother often, her father having moved back to England with another woman who, on the two occasions they had met, Anna hadn't liked. She wasn't sure how to talk of her pregnancy, or with whom. She knew that sooner or later she would have to, were she to keep the child.

In the eight years that had passed since Anna's father left, her mother had solidified. Throughout university Anna had half expected a second phone call to echo the first, her mother falling apart after her father's leaving. But the call never came, and Anna watched her mother slowly steady herself, taking that extra breath before replying, swallowing whatever sadness she had to to keep going. Anna's choice to study Beckett as an undergraduate was arbitrary, unaimed; but by the time of her PhD she experienced his writing as prophetic, as the voice her mother strangled in those breaths. *It is better to adopt the simplest explanation, even if it is not simple, even if it does not explain very much.*

She told her mother as little as she could, the bare facts, stripped of emotional judgement. Anna had prepared herself for an onslaught, for the full weight of her mother's unspoken anger at her father's betrayal to fall on her, or on Orr, whom she did not name. But Anna's mother responded to the news with a quiet pragmatism. She arranged doctor's appointments, made lists of baby items that she would need, even began preparing a room in her house where Anna and the baby could stay. The expected interrogation did not come, and Anna felt, in a strange way, disappointed. She had wanted conflict, something to react to and fight against, and neither Orr nor, now, her mother would provide it.

It was terrifying, Anna said later, that it was not terrifying. That it felt so natural, making and carrying a child inside her with a man she did not know she could trust, or rather, that she knew she could trust to be exactly and entirely himself, whatever that was, but who in some distinct way *was not hers*. Possession obsessed her in those first few weeks. Who belongs to whom, and in what way can human beings belong to one another, or, for that matter, to themselves? She had not, until a child grew in her womb, thought of relationships as a form of property, but now she could think of nothing else. She returned repeatedly in her head to Beckett's description of love in *Malone Dies* as 'a kind of lethal glue', and lay awake at night – on her back, a new, forced position – trying to imagine what it would be like, holding her own child in her arms. In these visions, Orr hovered in the background, present but out of focus, addendum. She could see, she claimed, the child's face before it was born.

She found herself not so much embracing the idea of motherhood as falling into it. It was not a pile of books beside the bed, or signing up for classes, but a simple quality of attention: she *noticed* children in a way she had, she realised for the first time, never done before. They *existed*. She began to see what had always been there. It came as a shock. She who thought she was so observant, so sharp and precise, had failed utterly to register the presence, the *interiority*, of so many people. Interiority, yes: the inner life, the racing thoughts and unfolding trauma of human existence, pounding itself into the future heartbeat by heartbeat as they clattered and thrashed their way around her. On one afternoon, as she walked through the Botanic Gardens after work – the gardens sat adjacent to the university, and on sunny summer evenings when the students had largely evacuated the city they were populated by families, old couples, the great unwashed of Belfast – she spotted a young girl chasing a butterfly. It was a clichéd delight, her tiny arms flapping and her cheers and shrieks as the butterfly dipped and hovered, moving from leaf to leaf. But Anna watched with something close to horror as she saw the child learn – in a matter of minutes – that if she was quieter, and slower, and more deliberate, the butterfly would not move so readily. That it could be, in a word, fooled. The girl's eyes narrowed, her face tightened into a furrowed, vital concentration; Anna saw her lose her sense of everything else in the park and become a composed, taut violence, poised to pounce. And she did pounce, and caught the butterfly, and in catching it crushed it. Anna stared at her as she stared at the broken creature in her hand. Her face relaxed again into a calm flatness, and she beheld the deadness with absolute impassivity. And then she shook it off, and turned before it had even hit the ground, laughing and running back to her parents, sitting forty feet away, oblivious.

Anna was beginning to show; a hint of roundness to her belly, a faint pulsing in her body which she may, she thought, have been imagining. It was a period of silence, of a sort.

Sarah left the house, a bright June day, heat in the air from early morning. The three boys had left for school already. Orr was in his study, and heard the front door open and close. He turned to the window to see her walk down the driveway. She worked as a teaching assistant in a primary school in Holywood, just outside Belfast. Orr watched her go, as she did every morning, to walk to the station.

At two-thirty Orr's phone rang. He was in the hospital visiting an elderly member of the congregation. He ignored it. It rang again, the same unknown number, and he excused himself and stepped out of the room. The caller identified himself as Superintendent Murphy from Bangor Police Station, and asked if he was speaking to Samuel Orr. We need you to come to the hospital, said Murphy. I'm in the hospital, said Orr. There was a brief moment of confusion, after which Murphy said, Your wife has been involved in an accident. You need to come to the Royal. Orr said, I'm in the Royal, Ward 34. Where is she? Is she alright? Come to A&E, said the policeman. Now.

Orr stepped back into the old man's room, made a brief apology, and walked quickly to A&E. By the time he arrived he was running. There were two policemen standing with a doctor. He described what happened, on the few occasions he talked of it at all, less as a story than a list, as things observed: the senior policeman, Murphy, a good fifteen years older than himself; moustache; younger partner doesn't introduce himself; doctor, forties, wears a name tag: Dr Susanna Bell; small amount of blood on her jacket sleeve, glistening; follow me, she says (like Jesus); Murphy nods to his colleague.

You can almost see him, walking behind her as she strides quickly through the overlit corridors of the emergency wards. She opens a door and steps inside. The light comes on by itself, a sick green hue. An office, not a ward room; Orr feels his stomach turn. Take a seat, Mr Orr, she says. Orr shaking his head, struck dumb. Your wife was hit by a train. She died there. At the station. Silence. It seems she slipped as the train approached the platform at Holywood. Silence. I'm sorry. Silence.

He asks to see her, and when they initially refuse – she was mangled, broken in a way a body should not be – he insists. When they pull the sheet back he says nothing. The policemen and the doctor recede. Orr's heart quickens, pounding so hard he can feel it against his chest. A train hurtling at speed, the pull of air as it passes, part gravity and part desire. He feels himself pulled forward, towards the body. He feels the panic rise in his throat, imagines faces at the window watching for a reaction. Sounds compounding, adding one on top of the other, until the silence is a roar. He stares at the body until the noise abates, fights with himself until the only sound he hears is not a sound at all but a question, which he knows will never now be silenced: did she really slip? *When nothing is named, confusion grows and with it comes anguish.* What name could he give it? Naming is a presumption, an act of ownership. But there is nothing to own; an absence, a place where something used to be.

Sarah's father, Jackie, ran a grocer's on the Cregagh Road, the same shop he'd owned since Sarah was born. Orr called him, and he closed the shop early – it was only four in the afternoon – and made his way to the Royal. Jackie did not know about Orr's affair. He hugged Orr to his chest, something he'd never done before. It was like holding a greyhound, he said: coiled energy, all blood and muscle. Jackie spoke to the doctor, and Orr sat by himself, still, staring ahead. Jackie called Orr's parents, who arranged to pick the boys up – the two youngest, both still at primary school, had been waiting for over an hour for their mother. He brought Orr to the hospital café for food. You can't just stay here, he eventually said to Orr, who had hardly spoken since Jackie arrived. I'll drive you home.

Orr resisted. He drove himself home, despite Jackie's protests, and spent the night alone. He texted Anna only to say that he wouldn't be there to visit her the next day. Orr was not given to texting, and Anna was unsettled. She called him immediately but he did not answer.

It was three days before Orr saw Anna. She knew already. The news report had been specific, and whilst Anna had

deliberately avoided learning the detail of Orr's domes-
tic life, she immediately recognised the name and the
geography. She called him again – this was the day after
the accident – and offered awkward, hesitant sympathies.
Guilt had not been a stranger to either of them; Anna had
cocooned it within her, hedged it off with a combination
of Orr's brazen example and her own visceral, physical
pleasure. But for the first time it took on a substance, it
ceased to merely hover in the background of their love
but stepped into full view. Anna found herself touching
her belly constantly, as though the innocence of the child
might somehow be transferred to her. Or vice versa.

For the three days Orr remained cut off, sealed inside
his own world. He moved between his house and the
paths across Divis and Black Mountain, pacing out his
grief and anger and whatever else ran nameless through
him. The rain fell persistently, the sky low and full.
His children stayed with his parents. He phoned on the
second day, and his mother told him that he must come
to them, that they needed their father now. But he did
not go, not until the following afternoon. He walked
through his parents' unlocked front door, into the living
room, where they sat blankly watching television. The
youngest child was five years old; his face was red from
crying. None of them moved when he entered the
room. He kissed each of them on the head, then turned
off the television and sat in an armchair facing them.
For a moment they simply stared at him. You know
your mother is dead, he said finally. But we are alive.
The youngest had stopped crying, and like the other
two, watched him, followed his eyes and words with

expectation. Orr's father had also come into the room, but Orr didn't acknowledge him. The boys looked at him without fear. I love you, Orr said to them. The youngest stood up, still tearless, and put his arms around his father, and Orr responded, and there was a stillness, and death was temporarily defeated.

But only temporarily. As Orr himself had often preached, the dead do not stay dead. He called on Anna that evening, the third day. She opened the door to him and wordlessly touched his face. Her hands moved over the surface and he closed his eyes. *And the earth was without form, and void; and darkness was upon the face of the deep. And the Spirit of God moved upon the face of the waters.* He opened his eyes and she led him inside. They sat in the kitchen and drank tea, the rain finally stopped, the late light of summer throwing lines on the table, like the bars of a prison cell. They barely spoke. Orr remained inaccessible, present but detached. She wanted to ask him what would happen next, but the questions dissipated as they formed, each insufficient to the moment and to what it was she really wanted; not information, but Orr himself.

They slept together, though they did not have sex. The alteration: first one held, then the other; an exchange of griefs and fears. There was a hesitation, as though they were sharing the same words but in a different language that neither had quite mastered. Anna's sleep was broken; every hour or two she stirred. But each time she found Orr sleeping, his face a stone.

In the morning, as Orr dressed, she said to him, God did not do this.

He was silent, putting on his clothes. Then he nodded.
No. We did.

On the following Sunday Orr did not preach. He sat in
the church like everyone else, in a seat a few rows from
the front, and listened to the words of a young man barely
out of school tell of the great things the Lord had done
for him. Everyone knew of Sarah's death. The boys sat by
Orr, in order of height, eldest to youngest. It was a sight
rarely seen, as Orr was almost always at the front, con-
ducting affairs, and the boys sat with their mother. The
effect of the four of them together was almost startling,
their features so similar that it looked as though, if one
said something, all their mouths would move together.

At the end of the meeting people lingered, reluctant to
leave; Orr was hugged and touched and left in no doubt
that the pain he was feeling was shared. The boys stood
beside him, receiving the same attention, though many
of the men weren't sure how to engage them and some
ruffled their hair with a sympathetic pat, which Philip
quickly tired of. The youngest did not cry, had not cried
since Orr's return. He stood implacable like a soldier
returned from war, soaking up sympathy, no longer able
to be surprised or saddened.

The days that followed were full of activity. The inevitable involvement of a coroner meant that Sarah's body
was not released for burial until the Tuesday, and so the
funeral was scheduled for Thursday, over a week after she

died. Those days lay before Orr like a minefield; Anna had never seen him so uncertain, so self-conscious. She had been, up to this point, drawn to his confidence, his seeming solidity, but she found this other, vulnerable Orr just as compelling. It unnerved her, this realisation; that this man could fall apart completely and she would still love him. It was like a power, or possibly a weakness, she never knew she had, a capacity for desire that seemed increasingly unconcerned of an object.

They saw each other only once more before Sarah was buried. On the day before the funeral the boys were still staying with Orr's parents, and Orr visited Anna. They went for a walk together along the towpath by the Lagan, where summer was in full, fecund display. It was early afternoon when they set out, the sun throwing short shadows around them, Anna slightly rounded in the middle, her clothes almost ready to be exchanged for the loose drapes – curtains, she called them in one of her later poems – that would hide and show her growing belly. They were comfortable in silence, and needed to be, and they walked without touching. Anna asked him how he prayed.

Do you mean how can I pray at a time like this, or what way do I actually do it? Orr asked.

Both.

I do it by just talking. Sometimes I close my eyes, sometimes I don't. That's not a metaphor, he almost smiled.

And how do you pray? she asked again.

Orr was silent for a long time and then said, simply, We're in this together.

Anna was unsure if the *we* meant herself and Orr, or herself and Orr and God, or – and this possibility only came to her much later – just Orr and God.

The funeral was small and private. The story had made the news, but Orr was left, along with his congregation and friends, to mourn in peace. The service was in the mission hall, and was presided over by an older pastor from another church in the country, who had known Orr since he was a boy. He spoke with deliberation and a marked, steady rhythm which lifted and fell as he praised the young woman whose body lay in the coffin before them, but whose soul was already in the arms of her saviour. He read from Isaiah 55: *For my thoughts are not your thoughts, neither are your ways my ways, saith the Lord. For as the heavens are higher than the earth, so are my ways higher than your ways, and my thoughts than your thoughts.*

Orr stood up to speak about his wife. For my thoughts are not your thoughts, neither are your ways my ways, he repeated. He spoke awkwardly, hesitating, stumbling from one word to the next. The calmness, the measured precision deserted him, and he spoke as though grasping, still looking for the words as he said them.

The coffin was carried for about a quarter of a mile, up the Beersbridge Road to the junction with Bloom-field, where it was lifted into the hearse. Orr and Philip shouldered the front, with four men from the church behind. Philip was not as tall as his father, but insisted that he be allowed to be one of the bearers, and they placed two cushions on his shoulder to help keep the height uniform. At the graveside the visiting pastor read the words of the apostle: There is one glory of the sun, and another glory of the moon, and another glory of the stars: for one star differeth from another star in glory. So also is the resurrection of the dead. It is sown in corruption; it is raised in incorruption: It is sown in dishonour; it is raised in glory: it is sown in weakness; it is raised in power: It is sown a natural body; it is raised a spiritual body.

They lowered the coffin into the ground and Orr threw mud on it. Two men from the council filled up the hole as the mourners left. Philip stood alone, face marked from earlier tears, watching them.

After the funeral there was a small gathering at the mission hall, where food had been prepared by some of the older women. The atmosphere was subdued, constricted, the grief different in its contours than at other funerals they had all witnessed. Sarah was so young, there was no escaping the sense of a brokenness in the order of things which lingered among the mourners even after the consolation of the scriptures. It was coupled with the sense that Orr's charisma, his simple ability to put others at ease, seemed to be working in reverse, and the gap between the Orr they had known and this new Orr – an Orr who did not even seem to know how to do grief properly – was too confusing. People drifted away quickly. His parents eventually left with the boys, and the handful of mourners who remained began packing away food and stacking chairs. Orr and the visiting pastor

stood off to the side for a long time, Orr doing the listening, his face towards the floor. The older man eventually
put his hand on Orr's shoulder, and said goodbye.

Orr visited Anna the following night, and she asked him
about the funeral. He described it for her, his tone flat
but containing a calmness too, a warmth that seemed
to be spreading inside him, as though the old Orr was
considering returning, testing the waters. She was overwhelmed by, at first, a blunt satisfaction, which turned
almost instantly to shame at her own callousness. Sarah
was in the ground less than a day, and Anna already
found that she could not help but feel glad, or, if not glad
exactly, relieved, that the unsettled question of ownership was suddenly in her favour.

As he was leaving he put his hands on her belly, just as
he had when she had announced she was pregnant. She
put her hands on top of his, and looked at his face, but
his eyes stayed where they were, directed at her belly, at
the child within. He shook his head.

What? she asked him. What is it?

Without looking up he answered, If I do not love you
I shall not love.

He kissed her and Anna watched him leave, considering for the first time that the line was perhaps as much
threat as promise.

III

Orr took a month off from his pastoral duties after the funeral. The boys returned home, and it was now Orr's responsibility to ensure they were dressed, fed, taken to school. There was some relief for Orr in this, the distraction of routine, but the boys struggled to adjust. Their father had been present and affectionate in their daily lives from the beginning, but this was a new form of intimacy, and neither they nor Orr knew how to move into it. The middle child adapted most quickly. His needs, perhaps, their uncomplicated flatness – an eight-year-old with simple desires and the language to express them – left space that Orr could fill with relative ease, whereas the other two fought much harder to work out what they needed or wanted from him. The youngest had stopped crying, but a dull stoicism took root in its place, a loss that he was old enough to experience but insufficiently able to articulate, and it began to mark a pattern he would never shake. Philip, on the other hand, had been the confidant of his mother, and Orr was never certain how much she had told him before she died, how many words he had stored up inside, many (perhaps) against his father. He offered no hint of this to Orr, and Orr worried that to question the boy might feel like an intrusion on a grief to which he had no right. And so they walled themselves in, and lost each other. Orr, in fairness, had Anna. Philip had no one.

The school holidays arrived in the first week of Orr's month off, so he had little time to himself. The two older boys went to a sports scheme in a local leisure centre with other children from the area, and Orr and the youngest would spend the day together. At first Orr tried to read or study in the mornings while the child watched television, but when Orr sat down with him on one occasion and experienced the inanity of the shows for himself, he decided they should go out for walks instead. They visited local parks, and occasionally Orr would drive somewhere further, the Waterworks in the north of the city or the Pickie Pool in Bangor where pedalos in the shape of swans could be rented for a few pounds. Twice a week Orr left him with his parents, and travelled across the city to Anna. The immediacy of the passion had diminished, but they were both, Anna felt, finding their way into a new connection, and she was not concerned. The question of what would happen when the child came lay between them unasked; conversation by conversation they circled it, coming ever closer. It was unusual for Orr, Anna was aware, to be so indirect.

It is not hard to imagine the thoughts that surely hovered in Orr's mind during this time. His life, which had only months before seemed so regimented and purposeful, now lay riotously, terrifyingly open. It was clear that he would have to tell the members of his congregation, though when and how, and how much, remained uncertain.

The day before he was to return to the mission hall, to resume his duties and preaching, Orr asked the elders for an extra two weeks off. He promised them that he would not need any further time beyond this fortnight, but that he needed to take a trip, that there were conversations with God he needed to have before he would be ready to continue. The two weeks were granted, and his parents again agreed to take the boys. His father was not convinced. He had begun to poke at the edges of Orr's moods to see what lay there besides grief. Orr knew how to bear a silence, had learned it, indeed, from his father. He told him he was going back to Elgin, to where he had first been saved.

His father wondered aloud at the wisdom of this. God is not found in a place but in our hearts, he said.

Yes, said Orr, but sometimes he hides.

God never hides, his father said. The blindness must be yours.

Orr nodded. Perhaps it is both.

Orr's father, Adam, was a complicated man. Raised by a dour Scottish Calvinist who moved to Belfast as a teenager and became a skilled carpenter in the shipyard, not long after the success and tragedy of the *Titanic*, he had grown up with a curtailed joy at the world, tasting everything bitter. The old man had never really adjusted to Belfast life, his teenage Scottish burr a permanent hindrance he deliberately refused to soften, and Adam inherited not only a hint of the accent, but something of his inability to be satisfied. Born unexpectedly in his father's forty-first year, he grew up surrounded by a voice constantly seeking grounds for disapproval, and, more often than not, finding them. Adam was an excellent footballer, and for a while it looked like he might make it across the water, to one of the big English clubs. But a bad knee injury in his late teens put paid to that dream, and he ended up stuck in the postal service, delivering mail in south Belfast, never quite able to shake the disappointment of an unlived life. Like his father he was saved, but regarded Orr's role as a pastor with some suspicion, a combination of pride in his calling and scepticism that such a calling was necessary. He went to a different mission hall, one without a pastor, where the congregation sat around a table with bread and wine at the centre, and anyone – any man – could, at the prompting of the Holy Spirit, stand and speak. When Orr had told him of his decision to become a pastor, giving up his job as a mechanic, Adam had reacted at first with anger. Orr was only twenty-eight himself, with a two-year-old son, and Adam could not hide his frustration, though what the frustration was about, exactly, he would have been hard put to say.

Orr left for Elgin, despite his father, and spent his days moving between the mountains and the small seaside towns of Aberdeenshire. He called Anna only once, as he had said he would. He talked to her of the huge sky, of the summer light extending late into the day, turning the mountains incrementally from green to purple, shade by shade, and eventually to black, their forms seeming to grow heavier as darkness fell. He walked and walked, he told her, and laughed as he described finding God through his feet, a phrase that stuck with Anna and that she flirted with some years later, in a series of poems which took her as close as she ever came to an idea of spiritual transcendence in her writing. (It is no coincidence that the phrase itself is so material, so human; Anna flirted only with an earthbound God.)

Anna remained patient. It is true that Orr had lost his wife, and the attendant grief – and, as Anna alone knew, guilt – demanded of him a certain wrestling, which Anna understood he must do alone. But she was pregnant with his child, over halfway by this stage, and her life was about to change irreparably. Her mother asked her, only once, about this. Anna told her simply that it would be alright. The child in my belly, she said, is a kind of peace. Orr will be Orr, she said. But I am not carrying Orr, I am carrying my child.

Orr returned from Scotland with a renewed vigour. The hesitation had gone, and it seemed he had removed his guilt, whatever there was, shed it as a snake sheds its skin. He went to Anna as soon as he returned, straight from the ferry.

We are having a child, he said to her, as though revealing some new information, and when she didn't reply, he said, We should raise him together.

Him? Anna asked.

Yes, said Orr.

Anna nodded. Okay, she said. Let's raise him together.

On the following Sunday, the first in September, Orr stood up in front of the congregation. The two younger boys were not there, but Philip sat at the front. It was a wet, miserable day, the sky dull and grey, the rain audible on the roof of the hall. It was his first time back in the pulpit since the events of the summer, and a hushed, nervous energy passed invisibly from row to row, each scrape of a chair, each cough magnified and obvious. He spoke clearly, his voice sure.

I have been the pastor of this congregation for more than ten years. God has blessed me, and us, in many ways during this time, and together we have wrestled with his presence, and occasionally his absence.

A pause. Orr steadying himself.

I have stopped hearing his voice. Or, perhaps, I have stopped listening. Eight months ago I fell in love with a woman who was not my wife. She is called Anna. In a few months she will have a child. My child. I am no longer going to be your pastor. I have no right to speak to you of what God wants when I no longer know myself. I would like to tell you I am sorry for what I have done, but that would not be the truth.

The rain on the roof seeming heavier, like stones falling.

I told my wife three weeks before she died. If God has intended to punish me, he has succeeded. Though his cruelty seems to have lost its focus.

Orr sat down. The silence gave way to murmurs and confusion. No one knew what to do, where to look. Orr was sitting on a chair behind the pulpit. He looked at his son, sitting ten feet away. Philip stared at his father for ten, fifteen seconds, then simply stood up and walked out. No one else moved; they watched him walk down the centre of the hall. A dog barked in a nearby street, aggressive and pained. Philip opened the door without turning around, stepped outside, and pulled it shut behind him. The sound of the door seemed to act as a trigger. One by one the congregation stood up, some shaking their heads, and moved in silent, solemn procession to the door, following the boy. Orr watched them leave, refusing to hang his head, defiance to the end. Two minutes passed, three, five, until there was only a handful of people left, spread throughout the room.

An old man, Hugh Roddy, was still there; he had been a member of the congregation his whole life, had watched hundreds of people find Jesus, and community, in the same seats that now sat empty around them.

Will you lead us in prayer before you go, pastor? he said simply.

Orr stood up, and waited silently for a moment, enough time for any of those remaining to leave. None did. Our father who art in heaven, Orr began, moving his way unhurried through the Lord's Prayer. Lead us not into temptation, he said, and paused, and then continued, his voice unbroken.

The elders accepted Orr's resignation, and arranged to meet with him during the week. Orr was, of course, being paid by the congregation, and there was some debate as to how this state of affairs should be handled, not only in terms of the future – which was hardly in question, he would be paid nothing from this point on – but also the past.

On the following evening, the day before the arranged meeting, Roddy knocked on Orr's front door. Orr welcomed him without fuss. Over a cup of tea, Roddy explained that there were a number of elders who were out for blood, that he must be aware.

What am I supposed to do? asked Orr.

Contrition, said Roddy.

Orr stared at his tea for a moment, and set it down on the table. But I am not contrite, he said. I have stood before God for almost a year, wrestling with a love I have no words for, nor defence against. You feel I should have been stronger.

Roddy interrupted him. Not stronger. Just more honest.

There are different kinds of truth, Orr said.

Orr told Anna about his admission, his declaration. She said little, believing that this part of Orr's world, or what had been Orr's world, was intimately his, and should remain his. There was a dull fear buried somewhere inside her that the removal of Orr from his church would do something irrevocable to him, would destroy him in some subtle, contagious way, and that the very freedom that had opened up the possibility of their being together may yet be a disaster. But she kept it hidden, not only from Orr but from herself; even in her notebooks refusing it the words she would later use with the brutality of hindsight. She was pregnant, she figured; such a feeling could just as easily be the baby shifting, and she gave herself over to this wisdom, this cause.

His parents called on him on the Tuesday morning. The children had left early, Philip walking his brothers to their school before catching the bus to his own. Philip's anger had not diminished, but he had, at only twelve years old, already the wit and cruelty to refuse it an outlet. He answered his father's questions practically and politely, the slow rage inside him just a shadow of what it would become, and Orr was helplessly aware of the boy's solitude, if not the extent of his growing hatred.

His parents knew the basic outline, though not from Orr himself. They had heard through friends of his revelation at the mission hall, and moved from anger to anger at the various betrayals – of Sarah, of the boys, of themselves. By the time Orr sat down with them his father's mind was already made up, and Orr's telling of his story was of less interest than the pronouncement of his own judgement. Orr soaked it up, and then asked simply if they would continue to help with the boys. His father seemed taken aback, as though he had expected Orr to fight his corner, but his mother nodded and said simply, Of course.

Orr was not contrite, but he was sufficiently politic to know when to speak and when to remain silent. His meeting with the elders was short, and the result was

the revoking of Orr's leadership – which had already
been agreed – and the removal of all financial support
from that moment forward. No reference was made to
his past salary; Roddy, Orr later learned, was respon-
sible for this. His membership was viewed differently
from his leadership, and Roddy emphasised that as far
as they were concerned, Orr continued to be a member
of the congregation and a child of God, and what he
decided to do with that was very much up to him. As
he left the meeting Roddy took him aside and, without
speaking, pressed a book into his hands. It was a copy
of Kierkegaard's *Fear and Trembling*. When he got home,
he opened the book and found four fifty pound notes,
bookmarking a highlighted passage: *One became great by
expecting the possible, another by expecting the eternal; but he
who expected the impossible became greatest of all.*

Sarah's family ignored him. Orr heard through reliable
sources that Jackie, her father, had to be talked down
from violence. He may have been older, but he wanted
to cause Orr pain with his hands. And Orr would have
let him, or so he said. But wisdom, or whatever else it
could be called, prevailed, and Orr was simply ignored.
Their access to their grandchildren was conducted via
his parents, a palatable alternative.

Anna recalled the months that followed as though
watched through glass. They were all – herself, Orr,
the boys, his parents – struggling for definition, the
lines between things blurred and improbable. Within a
week of leaving the mission hall, Orr was working in a

small mechanic's yard off a side street near Orangefield. A young man he had worked with before becoming a pastor – a boy at the time, really, who went by Magee, although his real name was Jonny McGaughy – now ran his own business, and gave Orr the job out of a sense of obligation for the old days, when Orr had trained him with patience and humour. It had been years since he had worked on cars in any serious way, but he picked it up again quickly, and Magee was very quickly grateful not only for Orr's skill as a mechanic but for his way with people, an ease the younger man had never mastered. Orr, for his part, showed no hesitation or despondency at the change, indeed began to enjoy leaving work at three o'clock every day having finished something: replaced a steering column, fixed a gearbox, changed a set of brake pads. Most customers knew nothing of his recent story, of course, and bantered with the casual irreverent cheek so common in Belfast. But a few recognised him, and nudged their way towards the question of his new situation. Orr gave nothing away, and one or two must have left with imaginations already turning over as efficiently as their engines.

Orr collected the younger boys on his way home. He would make dinner as they did schoolwork or played, and he found another surprising satisfaction in preparing food. Philip would arrive home later, and continued to play the game: a contrived obedience, just the right side of what Orr demanded, but holding enough back to ensure that the disdain was visible. He took to singing absurd phrases around the house ('Holy, holy, holy Moses'), sufficiently weird to be noticed but not so much as to provoke a response, as though testing the limits of permitted blasphemy. Orr recalled one particular occasion when Philip walked in on him reading the Bible to his youngest son. He stared at them both briefly with, for the first time, undisguised fury, then walked out, the door echoing, a 'Fuck Jesus' hanging (possibly? probably?) in the air behind him.

Anna and Orr together were finding a new rhythm, an unspoken pattern. The fuel that had driven their earlier engagement, that blend of raw physical desire and longing, had been replaced with a subtler, slower humour. Where once they had come at the same time, Anna told her mother, typically without candour, they now laughed at the same time, and for now it was enough. Orr was present again, increasingly so as the weeks passed, and together they found, to their slight surprise, that the bringing together of their lives was not so very difficult.

It was not entirely without incident. Orr brought his youngest boys to her house to meet her (Philip refused to go, and Orr did not push the issue). They were well raised, polite children, their natural boisterousness contained in a discipline that both Orr and Sarah had managed uniformly. Even still, as they stood before Anna for the first time some hesitation seemed to catch in them, and they stared without speaking, until the youngest said simply and without malice, as though in answer to some unasked question, My mummy is dead. She went to heaven.

As the visits played out week by week, they grew used to Anna, and came, maybe, to love her. She had no desire to mother them, and this space she allowed, this refusal of her own authority, opened up a way to a kind of affection, she felt, in both directions, which might otherwise have been impossible. On occasions they went out together, to visit the museum or see the new *Titanic* building, and Anna would catch a glimpse of them all in the mirror of an exhibition case and experience a confusion of emotion, an uncertainty as to what exactly she was looking at, as though they themselves, their twisted little family, were on display. She asked Orr about it one night before he left – he always returned home to the boys, never spent the night – and he smiled and said, as though he had been preparing for just this kind of question, There are stranger genealogies than this one.

Philip was not part of this picture, but his absence was never unmarked. He hovered around Orr; the more he pulled away the more Orr would sense him, as though they were invisibly but physically connected. Philip, Anna sensed, was standing in for Orr's own guilt. He became the embodiment of his angst, to the extent that Orr began to believe, though he would never say as much, that he must either bring Philip close or get rid of him. Anna did not share her suspicions with Orr, and wondered later what would have happened if she had; perhaps she could have headed something off, defeated fate by naming it in advance.

At the time, however, Philip and Orr staked out their territory. Philip was not yet a teenager, and Orr a grown man. And yet some people bring a skill to punishment, and Philip moved into it as though it were a calling. In the four years that followed there was virtually no respite. Philip became a master of self-control, of the refusal of his own satisfaction. He felt that were he to enjoy himself it would let Orr off the hook, would allow Orr to feel that the damage he had wrought was *within limits*; and so he denied himself happiness in order to ensure that his father would not for a moment relax, never even once be able to convince himself that what had occurred had ended. Philip *became* continuation, the past blurred into the present. It was like the story they told children: if you pull a face and the wind changes direction it stays that way for ever.

Anna wrote, much later, that we grow like trees rather than animals; that that which distorts and hurts us is not shaken off a day, a week, later, but twists and gnarls, forcing us into further distortions, further convulsions of form. It is language, she said, that performs this dubious service. The other animals remember wordlessly, an instinct primed for fear or desire; they move faster or slower, senses heightened, ears pricked, their whole body an impression. But we humans build stories, throw words at our experiences until they harden, and branch after twisted branch, God help us, we grow into the sky and into the ground.

An illustration. A couple of years later, when Philip was fourteen, he began to have nightmares, dreams of hell, devils and fire and convulsions. His bedroom shrank, or expanded, to the size of Dante's circles, and night after night he would wake up gasping, the shrill sounds of the mocking demons still ringing in his ears. Orr went in to him, sat on his bed, and Philip slowly calmed down, his soft heart thumping, though his face retained some of the fear of the images so recently forced upon him. He was freezing cold, but would not let Orr touch him. But he did not make him leave the room, and for almost two months the pattern played out, three or four times a week, Orr sitting on his bed, light from the landing falling across his back, and Philip in the darkness, finding himself again. It was not lost on Orr: *The Lord is longsuffering, and of great mercy, forgiving iniquity and transgression, but by no means clearing the guilty, visiting the iniquity of the fathers upon the children unto the third and fourth generation.* Orr realised for the first time its brutal truth: not as proscription, but observation. He had given his child this gift, and he could not take it back.

Still, the fact that Philip allowed Orr to sit beside him, silently on his bed, began to compensate. He felt, finally, a thawing, a window opening into his son's life. And it was this that brought the nightmares to an end as abruptly as they had begun. It is testament to Philip's taste for control that whenever he realised Orr was gaining ground, as he lay at his weakest, exhausted and fearful on his own bed, that even then he found the strength inside him to defeat the demons, to chase them away, and to reinstate the distance from his father he had so carefully nurtured. There were no more sweats, startled shouts, clutching at air. When Orr looked in on him he looked like he was hardly breathing at all, as though the truest peace had suddenly enveloped him. But Anna believed he had simply made a decision. The demons had not gone away at all, his dreams still flooded

with hell. But he decided that he belonged there, that he
was, in a word, *home*.

I am getting ahead of myself.

On the morning of 4 January, Anna gave birth to a
son. They called his name Samuel, like his father, like
Beckett. He was almost two weeks overdue; perhaps he
knew what was coming. Orr was present at the birth,
held Anna's hand as the child emerged, its lungs already
primed, the blood of his mother a sticky, viscous coating.
Other animals lick it off; in the hospital they used soft
towels, and they wrapped him as he cried and placed him
on his exhausted mother's chest, feeling already for the
nipple, ravenous and new. Orr was outwardly calm, but
even in her tiredness Anna was aware of some brooding
undercurrent, a rip-tide pulling at him, as though the
whole event had been a surprise and only now was he
realising the magnitude of what was happening. Orr's
mother asked him what it was like, what it felt like,
holding his new son for the first time. Like fear, he said,
only stronger. Love, I suppose.

The child stayed in the hospital for a few days. The
birth itself had been uncomplicated, though the labour
was long and painful, and Anna struggled to sleep even
when it was over, the echoing sounds of the hospital
drifting into the ward, the blue of the ambulance lights
from the streets far below flashing faintly against the
windows throughout the night. But the child slept well,
and took to the breast with ease and greed. Orr visited

for as long as he was allowed on those first days, and even brought his children, Philip excepted, to see their new brother. Half-brother, Philip reminded him.

On the third day Orr drove Anna home, where her mother was waiting, food prepared for weeks in advance, a small crib for the baby which she had assembled herself. She welcomed them warmly; she had met Orr a number of times already, and had grown to like him, his sober humour a match for her own. Anna moved slowly but with strength growing daily, and they ate a first meal of soup and bread in a silence broken only by the noises of the child, whose presence filled the spaces they may otherwise have felt compelled to fill with words. Anna's mother had offered to move in for the first few weeks, and Anna had agreed, so Orr stayed for an hour and left. On the way out Anna said to him, We did it. He nodded, smiled, and replied simply, We did. When Anna closed the door it again struck her that perhaps they were not talking about the same thing.

The movement into motherhood, for Anna, was less like journeying into another country than like discovering in her own home a room she never knew existed, furnished already and comfortable. She noted that her senses changed, physically; her hearing became more acute, attuned to the sounds of her child's cries and movements. She was not nervous; as though the unlikelihood of how the child had come about was a confirmation that something – which she resisted naming – was on her side. Over the first few weeks as she held him, both part of herself and plainly other, the awareness of an observation began to grow in her, which she had had no anticipation of. As she grew accustomed to looking at him, the faces of others, even Orr himself, grew grotesque, ugly. They were outsized, the child's face the new measure of everything. She could trace it with her finger: initially the whole face fitting inside the palm of her hand as she held him to her breast, but day by day growing, pushing itself into the surrounding space, until other faces gradually retained their normality. Anna never forgot the sensation, however. Some new scale had been introduced to the world.

Philip resisted the overtures from his father to visit, and so, at two weeks old, he brought the child to him. Philip was sitting on his bed reading, and heard his father and brothers arriving home, but, as usual, ignored them. Orr opened the door to his bedroom, and Philip looked up as Anna brushed past Orr and sat on the edge of the bed, Samuel wrapped tight in her arms. Philip stared at them both, silent. Anna said, This is Samuel. She held the child out to Philip as Orr watched on, struck dumb by a genuine nervousness. Philip paused only for a few seconds and then reached out and lifted the child from Anna, accepted him, and held him close to his face, looking at him intently. The child wriggled in his hands. His eyes, so filled with a forced hatred, seemed to change colour, and he once again became, if only briefly, the child he was. In the position they were in, Samuel's back was to Anna, so she could not see his expression; but Philip's face became a mirror, following the child, chasing his smiles and grimaces. Orr's youngest moved beside Philip, nudging on to the bed, and Orr reached out his arm to steady him, to ensure he did not cause Philip to drop the child. It jarred Philip back to himself, the reminder that Orr was in the room, and he quickly handed Samuel back to Anna, nodding his head as though in answer to a question he had not been asked.

In the following weeks, and after Anna's mother had moved back home, a routine was established. Orr was more or less tied to his house, with occasional exceptions thanks to the generosity of his parents in looking after the boys, so Anna would stay with him four nights a week. Anna was hesitant at first. She was aware that she was moving into what had been Sarah's space, and knew that Orr would be subject to criticism that she may never hear but which would surely hurt him. But he dismissed this concern, moving with his typical disregard for the opinions of others into embracing the one practical option in front of them. He bought duplicates of each of the items the child would need and set up what had been his study as a nursery.

The boys responded in different ways to the new arrangement. The middle child embraced it wholeheartedly, giving himself over to his new brother as one might to a new toy. It can hardly be called luck, but there was something different about losing one's mother at eight years old, and not five or twelve. The youngest, although he had initially responded with excitement and affection, soon grew ambivalent, then actively hostile, as though he had belatedly realised that he had been usurped, and had even, somehow – his own kindness, perhaps? – hastened the situation he now resented. He retreated further into

himself, and engaged Samuel less and less. On one occasion, in the middle of the night, Orr awoke to find him
standing over Samuel's cot in the nursery, staring silently
at the sleeping child. Orr, no stranger to scepticism about
human nature and the potential for violence embedded
in even the most average of men, was struck suddenly
and for the first time that this tendency was as present, as
possible, in the rooms of his own house. It was concrete,
a brick in his chest, he told Anna some months later,
when the full visceral extent of the realisation had run
through him: depravity not as a moral failure, but as a
fundamental of childhood, as natural as smiling or lying
down, and no less enjoyable. Orr watched his new child,
and watched his other children watching his new child,
and his mind moved to places he had not been aware of,
images conjured seemingly out of nowhere but palpable,
fraught violence at their edges.

He had naturally assumed that the most worrying
demonstration of this would have been found in Philip;
so much groundwork had he already done, and there was
little subtlety to his disgust at his father, nor to the anger at
the new life foisted on him. And yet that first interaction
with Samuel, the child held in his arms as the others
watched, seemed to have worked in some indefinable
way, and Orr was fascinated, and wise enough to keep his
fascination hidden, with the way Philip began to move
into the child's orbit, began to watch for him and play
with him, to see him as – Anna used the word much later,
too much later, perhaps – an *accomplice*. Philip began to
treat Samuel differently from everyone else, and, within
the context of the family at least, to build his life around

the child's, as though he was the one tolerable part of the whole story. An affection developed between them, which moved in both directions. Philip was able to evoke reactions of wild humour, joy even, in Samuel that could not be replicated by either Orr or Anna, much to Orr's unease and Anna's amusement. They fell into a routine: Samuel launching objects across a room, discovering his arms; Philip, laughing, returning them, to coos of gleeful delight. A delight suspended, temporarily, when Orr arrived home from work one day to discover the missile being hurled was his bible.

Anna continued to write during this period, this first year of her child's life. She had been given two full semesters off teaching but had promised to turn in a number of papers for a Beckett conference in Barcelona towards the end of the year. Finding time to read had, naturally, become more difficult, and the mundane realities of raising a child, or, more accurately at this early stage, keeping a small creature alive and healthy, consumed her in a way she had not quite been prepared for. And yet she found herself returning to Beckett, when she could, with a renewed wonder, a feeling for the beauty in his blunt physical descriptiveness and obsession with the body, farting and fucking and so on, which, while it had once amused her, now moved her unexpectedly to pathos. She had never been one of those academics who look for clues as though they could unlock a text, render its meaning transparent and useful; but she was struck by the emotional reactions into which she found herself falling, to passages she had read dozens of times already but without the same impact. At first she was uncertain, self-critical, cautious of this access to her own inner world which seemed tangibly closer than it ever had before, as though it could not be compatible with the scholarly rigour to which she faithfully adhered. And yet the insights lingered, and formed a vocabulary of their own, and she began to embrace them as truths and build her new work around them.

During this first year more poems emerged. *Emerged*: her word; reluctant initially to own their authorship, she talked of them more like discoveries than creations. This was a self-conscious theme, rooted in her experience of giving birth to a child who she could not quite believe she had *made*, inside her body, out of pieces of – where are the lines drawn? – surely herself. This collection, eventually published a couple of years later, became a foundation of sorts. Anna found a facility with words, with their careful arrangement and occasional awkwardness, which gave some form to the impossibility of the last few years, the unaccountability of it all. She was not yet thirty, and her life had, it seemed suddenly, taken on a shape, an outline, which though entirely new felt concretely, if inexpressibly, *right*.

The ironies of this were not unmarked – she was constantly, ruthlessly aware of occupying a space that was not entirely hers. Sarah continued to inhabit the house, the colours of the walls, the curtains, the saucepans, all loaded with her decisions, her choices. Anna watched herself move between asserting her own presence and backing away from it; she was never more alert to her own desire than in those first months in Orr's (Sarah's) house. She bought new bedding, identical in colour and style to what had been there; Orr never remarked on it, and she never knew if he realised or not. She burned the original sheets in her back garden, watched the black smoke trail upward and disappear.

Orr was always supportive of Anna's writing. There was no mockery, no giving in to the vanity of seeing everything that is difficult to understand as irrelevant, or pretentious. Anna was tentative in these early creative forays, but gained confidence from the simple, direct encouragement Orr provided, his desire to hear her words slowly climb into sentences, into stanzas, colonising a whole page. She loved the strange, biblical poetry of his own speech, which still coloured his conversation despite his abandonment of the church.

She looked back later on these first poems as flat, too much compressed, too easily falling into an emotion that should have been restrained. But enough critics loved them, and a number were published in journals with a wide readership, gaining her a sudden if modest popularity. And despite her own harsh assessment, they held for her the rhythms of an astonishing period of her life, the intimations of which, she felt, filled the words, the lines, even the whiteness of the pages.

The child was healthy. Aside from a short bout of colic early on, during which he cried relentlessly – purposefully,

Anna wrote, unfairly – and a few common infections, he grew fast and strong. His appetite was vital; he fed hungrily, with evident satisfaction. He was inquisitive; Anna was struck by his strange tendency to listen to conversations, long before they could possibly make any sense to him. She had the uncanny impression, early on, when she would be talking with Orr while holding the child, that he was somehow taking it in, considering what was being discussed, as though storing it away for future consideration.

Orr continued to work, and with some success: after six months he was offered a partnership, but he declined. He talked it over with Anna, but it was clear that his mind was already made up. But the decision – the fact that he had to make a decision, to consider in a concrete, deniable way the future – turned something in him. An anxiety crept into his relaxation, arresting the edges of his sleep. He would wake in the night and peer about the room, as though looking for someone who had just addressed him. He smiled at Anna as he came around, softened, easing himself back to consciousness. But his face never quite composed itself fully, fraught now with a sensitivity to something, someone, hovering just out of frame.

The distance between Orr and Anna, initially narrowed by the presence of the child they had, between them, created, began to be reasserted by this same small, physical presence. Anna's touch became a site of contest. Orr would watch the baby on her breast, sucking hungrily, both drawn to and made uncertain by the sight. For Anna, the sheer physicality of her son was a startling location of pleasure, an eroticism she had not expected but found herself longing for daily, the strange combination of pain and focused, visceral pleasure as his mouth fastened on her, his rough gums on her nipples, first one then the other. On occasion, lying in bed, the sensation rose, spreading like melted butter, and she would orgasm, coming with a shudder, the child, oblivious, on her breast, still feeding. She wanted to tell Orr about this but felt she could not, that there was something too complicated for the kind of explanation he might require. And so she kept it to herself, in herself; and wondered, later, if this had been one of the tiny, invisible cracks that had formed beneath them, that she had in some silent way communicated this to him, some division, some resistance. If he had realised that with the arrival of the child he had, strangely, less of her than before. The sum was reduced.

Orr became distracted around Samuel, the uncomplicated attention he had given since the beginning dissolved in an uncharacteristic hesitancy. When minding him Orr had always resisted the garish ease of the television. But increasingly he would prop Samuel up on fat cushions in front of the screen and Anna would come home to find Orr in a different room, staring out the window. One miserable, wet day she returned to find Orr in the garden, drenched to the skin; the child had disappeared. They found him under the sofa, silent, content.

Anna knew something was approaching but she didn't know what it was. Orr pushed. Their intimacy grew more physical; she knew that the new pressure of his hands on her body, his rough tongue on her skin, held some unsaid, inarticulable truth. The pleasure of her coming, she knew as her limbs shuddered and contracted, held within it a truth that Orr was moving towards, or through, but as yet could not, or would not, bring himself to say. There were not many possibilities. They had never talked of marriage. She wondered briefly if he was wrestling with the question of whether or how to ask, but she dismissed the thought quickly, believing – rightly – that Orr would not have found this so demanding. When this realisation struck it was with a dull, breaking thud, and she knew what was coming with all the certainty of sin.

Anna was always so vigorous with her self-analysis, pitiless even. Still, who can avoid occasionally reading backward, events becoming signs becoming symbols, the inevitable unravelling of one thing before another, until the nod, the glance, the misplaced keys become augurs; history distilled to a hand raised at the wrong moment. Lowered at the wrong moment. One night, the child almost a year old, sleeping peacefully in the next room, Orr stood in the light from the bathroom and told her she must leave. Her and the child. Both of them. They must leave.

She did not leave. Not, at any rate, right away. I know you, she told him, and you do not mean this. Who are you to rid yourself of your child?

How can you know me if I don't know myself? was all he said, but he did not push the matter. They slept, untouching, for one night, and another.

Talk to me, she said. Tell me why. Show me what I have done.

But he wouldn't. He refused, simply, to touch her, until her body began to burn with the absence. The cruelty of his withdrawal, the impossibility of it, was brutal.

Still, she refused him the satisfaction. The boys watched them circle one another, trying to – as Anna wrote it – hurt one another enough to resurrect love.

You don't love me, she said.

I do, he said.

Is it because you feel guilty? That I am here, in this space? This space that isn't mine?

No, he said.

This is madness, she said finally, exasperated.

Yes, he said.

She packed her things in the middle of the day, in front of him. He watched her walk around the house, placing parts of her life into bags.

You need to be sure of this, she said.

He didn't reply.

The boys arrived home from school to see her car packed. Philip walked into the house like an animal after a kill, a poised, quiet stalking. He asked what was happening. Orr told him Anna was leaving. At first he assumed he'd won some sort of victory, his patience rewarded; but soon realised that this was his father's doing, complicating his satisfaction and blunting his brief joy. Samuel cried as she carried him out, as though aware that something significant was happening, some rending. The neighbours opposite, an older couple, stared shamelessly, faces distorted behind unwashed glass. Orr sent his boys inside.

Ask me to stay, she said.

Orr stared at her, silently.

She lifted Samuel into the car, the final piece of luggage.

Alright then, she said.

She stood in her kitchen, staring into the back garden. It was winter; the trees bare and diminished. It was hard to be certain that anything had really changed. She always returned to her own house a couple of times a week, slept there regularly; this was not a new geography. But she knew that something had broken, an unseen balance tipped. Her bags lay on the floor around her like dead animals. Sam had stopped crying, and was staring at her, reading her face, silent. She became aware of the light falling through the window and hitting the floor, and the small, humming mechanical noises, the everyday breathing of the house. She became aware of her own heart beating, could almost see in her mind the blood being pushed through her thin veins, the relentless trundling of it. It was all, suddenly, violent; forced. Nothing existed in itself, everything coerced, shoved around. There was nowhere to hide.

It is hard to know, even now, why Orr did it. He said once that he experienced God as a breath on his neck. *And, lo, I am with you always, even unto the end of the world*: an impressive threat. He did not see God in dreams, or hear a voice in his head and attribute it to heaven; he was fully aware that all the voices were his own, dripping with his own history. But it was in his body, and those of his children, even in the movement of an engine under his hands. For Orr God was everywhere and thudding, animate and warm, and his love as simple and repetitive as the silent hammer of the pulse under the skin, invisible and vital. It was not, I don't believe, that God told him to change his life; nor even a slow, steady accretion of layered guilt that finally overwhelmed him. But as Anna moved in his caresses, under his hands, he began to sense there an absence, a removal, and the deeper he went into it the further it receded.

Much later Anna wrote a poem, a long prose-poem of erasure, in which the words slowly disappeared, removed themselves from the page, until by the end of the book there was simply blankness, emptiness. And yet the emptiness was loaded, not empty at all, in fact, but heavy with absence, with implication. There is no nothing, there is never nothing; there are thousands and thousands and thousands of absences, myriad, a cacophony, relentless.

Anna spent Christmas at her mother's, with her son. She began to accommodate herself to the necessary contours of the coming days: the emptied-out uncertainty, the clean, repetitive loneliness. And she surprised herself by just how simple it was. The journey home from the university via her mother's house to pick him up, a meal alone, evenings spent writing, Sam asleep, and occasionally awake, in a cot beside her desk, tranquil, creation itself, glowing in candlelight. The emptiness just another routine to be performed.

As she considered it it was both comforting and troubling: that life could be so carelessly transformed, upset, and yet it persisted, continued seamlessly, and she did not fall apart. Her life – upset just as radically as Orr's – remained in some subterranean sense undisturbed. A river had burst its banks and flooded messily into the surrounding countryside, creating new rivers and streams and making old maps obsolete, but Anna's relation was to the water below, as wide and deep and hidden as it had ever been, unfazed by the newly disordered terrain. There was something steady in Anna, undeterred. A friend of her mother had visited during the holidays, whom Anna had not seen in many years, and remarked that as Anna had got older she had become more beautiful.

Anna smiled. Like a ruin, she said.

Orr went back to the mission hall. He had not returned since the morning he had made his confession, if confession is the right word, although Philip had continued to attend every week on his own, a complicated reminder of his father's absence. There is no nothing. Orr sat in the back row on the first Sunday, nodded when acknowledged by those on the seats around him. Philip had not expected to see him, and, sitting off to one side, stared at him throughout the service, God knows what unnameable emotions coursing through his young body.

It was Advent, and the text from Matthew's gospel gained weight, the words suddenly alive: Then said Mary unto the angel, How shall this be, seeing I know not a man? And the angel answered and said unto her, The Holy Ghost shall come upon thee, and the power of the Highest shall overshadow thee: therefore also that holy thing which shall be born of thee shall be called the Son of God.

Orr did nothing, of course; he did not actively *cause* the air to spark. But in his presence, the unfolding of the gospel acquired a penetration, an edge. The lines blurred. The infant Jesus was named, but only Orr's child, Orr's bastard, was imagined.

And then came the reading from Psalm 27:

A Psalm of David. The LORD is my light and my salvation; whom shall I fear? The LORD is the stronghold of my life; of whom shall I be afraid? When evildoers assail me, uttering slanders against me, my adversaries and foes, they shall stumble and fall. Though a host encamp against me, my heart shall not fear; though war arise against me, yet I will be confident. One thing have I asked of the LORD, that will I seek after; that I may dwell in the house of the LORD all the days of my life, to behold the beauty of the LORD, and to inquire in his temple.

Roddy watched the other congregants, stared at the faces of his fellow elders, and began to sense that what was happening in him, occurring to him, as he listened, was also happening to them. The psalm was talking about Orr: the lack of fear, the shaking off of slanders, the utter confidence, the steady desire (*to behold the beauty of the LORD, and to inquire in his temple*) was all Orr, was *in him*, present, alive. It had not gone away.

And more: that if it was in Orr, then perhaps Roddy and the rest were the evildoers, the adversaries and foes. If Orr still had God inside him, then who else were the host encamped against him, against whom his heart was not afraid, if not they themselves, the righteous judges? Roddy dismissed the thought as it flooded him, but it would not be so easily removed. Orr seemed to have an ability to make it *all about him*, to turn the scriptures into biography. And yet he did not actually do anything; he merely refused to change, to be anything other than his flawed, blunt self.

It is hard to know how Orr felt in all of this, what freedoms or fears he swallowed. Still, he returned, and it was natural, and there was no fanfare, nor – in public at least – recriminations. There were surely those who, in the privacy of their own homes, whispered their discomfort to one another. There was one family who left to attend another church some miles away, but for the most part the congregation opened to Orr and embraced him, tentatively but with genuine warmth.

For his part Roddy hesitated, torn between, on the one side, his Christian duty and his natural affection for Orr, and on the other his growing awareness of Philip's dissatisfaction, his – he would not have called it this at the time – hatred. Roddy was intent on Philip, noticing the concentration, the almost imperceptible shake of his hands when, a few weeks later, his father returned to the pulpit for the first time. Everyone else was watching Orr, watching his mouth form once again around the words of the prophet Isaiah:

Awake, awake; put on thy strength, O Zion; put on

thy beautiful garments, O Jerusalem, the holy city: for henceforth there shall no more come into thee the uncircumcised and the unclean. Shake thyself from the dust; arise, and sit down, O Jerusalem: loose thyself from the bands of thy neck, O captive daughter of Zion. For thus saith the Lord, Ye have sold yourselves for nought; and ye shall be redeemed without money.

Philip flinched, involuntary, as Orr found his rhythm; he leaned forward with shoulders strained, tight, as though against his own will. But he said nothing, made no protest. And he held his silence as week by week his father steadied himself, moved with quiet confidence back into his old pulpit. He had not been replaced in the year he was away, the congregation sharing the pastoral duties among themselves – their ability to do so testament perhaps to Orr's leadership, his ability to draw out of others what they might not have known was there – and within two months he was preaching again every Sunday. The sermons were not the same as before; they became more confessional and yet remained somehow impersonal, as though it was the text itself that was confessing, carrying a melancholy, a sense of loss which referred not, as it might once have done, to the distance between the listener and the text, but to some gap, some loss, *within* the text itself. Orr could never have been accused of avoiding the darker, more solitary avenues that faith occasionally takes, but his new persistence, his new pathways through the scriptures held some unnamed weight, force, which like gravity pulled the hearer in. When he preached of the man being let down through the roof to be healed by Jesus, Roddy recalled, you could feel the burn of the ropes in his friends' hands.

On a cold, wet morning at the end of January, during a term break at the university, Anna answered the door to Roddy. She had no idea who he was, and he stood uncomfortable on the doorstep, looking around him as though mistaken. Her initial impression was that an old man had lost his way. She waited for him to realise his error, but instead he asked, Are you Anna?

She brought him inside, and made tea. He sat in her kitchen, in the chair Orr had often sat in, and he seemed aware himself of the substitution, watching her with, as she imagined it, another's eyes; trying to put himself in Orr's position, to see what it was Orr saw. Anna was measured, reserved. It had been a month since she had seen Orr. He had come to her house on Christmas Day, and sat with the child on his lap, affectionate and warm. They did not talk much, but as he was leaving Anna asked him what was to happen next.

I need a few weeks, he had said.

A few weeks for what?

He shook his head, walked away. She had not seen him since, and had – as she had throughout the entire affair – continued in her own rhythm, the child's demands smoothing out the edges of each day, filling it and fattening it, so that the questions that played inevitably were quietened, softened.

Roddy told her that Orr had returned to the pulpit.

To the Lord? Anna asked.

Roddy smiled, wry. You'd need to ask him.

Which him? She tried to get a rise, but he didn't bite.

I've been a sceptic myself, he said.

Anna warmed to him immediately. Why are you here? she asked him. He would have told me himself.

Roddy nodded. I have no doubt, he said in reply. Still. I know what kind of man he is. I wondered if you'd been left on your own.

You know what kind of man he is? I imagine her looking at Roddy, squarely, as though assessing a piece of furniture she was considering purchasing. I'm not alone, I have the child.

Roddy nodded. Can I see him?

Anna carried Sam from the back room where he'd been sleeping and handed him, tightly bundled, to her visitor. She sat back in her seat and looked at them – Roddy cooing at the child, who reached his hands without fear to Roddy's lined face – and was overcome by a strange sense that they knew each other already, that in some other place, some hidden world, this infant and this old man were already joined, connected in a way beyond describing; and the impression, or more than impression, the conviction, the certainty, grew to encompass herself, absurd as it was, and for a moment the lines between them, the three of them, seemed entirely arbitrary, her own history accidental and contingent. It was not, she wrote, a transcendence, a movement out of the body; but more like an overfilling, a sense that the boundaries of the body itself were blurred, viscous, insufficient to the task of holding all that was within. It was all materiality, she said, the extraordinary weight of the ordinary.

It was a moment that passed quickly. But Anna was nourished by it, and it began, by her own account, to work something in her, some sense of herself, of her edges. What was it Beckett said about language? *To bore one hole after another in it, until what lurks behind it – be it something or nothing – begins to seep through; I cannot imagine a higher goal for a writer today.*

A week after Roddy's visit, Orr showed up. She opened the door, still in a dressing gown, and stared at him, his face unshaven but gleaming with some mischief. She wondered if he was drunk.

He came in and sat down. The child was asleep, so they sat alone in the kitchen, drinking tea. He stared out the window, looking at the trees he had once stared at from her bedroom, standing naked above. She wondered if he remembered this at all. She wondered if she should ask him.

I have not forgotten, he said, as though reading her thoughts.

What have you not forgotten?

He sipped from his tea, staring at her over the cup. I can't come back, he said.

You can do whatever you want, Anna replied.

Orr smiled and nodded, as though she had told a lie so blatant there was no need to refute it. Is that what your Beckett would say?

She considered calling him a coward, telling him he was hiding behind his God, putting words in God's mouth, denying his own responsibility to do as everyone must do and face the world in front of them, as it is, the blunt facts of solitary existence. She considered pointing out that his refusal to live with her and their child was a betrayal, a simple human betrayal, full of fear, utterly untouched by the divine. She considered staring at him in pity, pity so blunt he could not mistake it, shaking her head slightly from side to side, mocking him. She considered setting a bible in front of him and telling him to point out the bit where this happens, where God's wisdom floods a tiny Belfast kitchen with indifference, hostility, loneliness. She considered handing him the child, making him look at the boy and speak to him, to explain to him in terms he would one day understand. She did none of these things. Instead she repeated, again, as though he had not heard it the first time, You can do whatever you want.

Her refusal to confront him with her considered accusations was neither weakness nor fear; rather, she was not convinced that he was wrong. She had fallen in love with Orr in all his complication, all his ridiculous conviction, and it would have been a denial of this, she felt, to force him now to turn his back, to abandon the God he had thus far refused to abandon. It did not matter that she did not believe in this God herself; for her to change Orr would have been an act of sabotage, would have destroyed the very space out of which her love for him emerged. Anna's love for Orr required giving him up, handing him over to his God, and living with the consequences.

They came to an arrangement. Orr would see the child once a week, and contribute financially. But no official division of access was required: as far as Orr was concerned, Anna could raise him. Orr kissed the child, rubbed his soft blond hair, curling at the ends, and walked away. He moved to kiss Anna also, dipping forward towards her cheek, but she stepped back and stared at him, refusing either him or herself, or both, whatever satisfaction there may yet have been. He let himself out, and she stared at the space he had vacated, his absence, and finally – for the first time – she cried. There had been no surprise, nothing had been revealed that she had not already seen, but the completeness of it, the mathematical nature of the agreement they had come to, was suddenly so ugly, so crude, that the child, staring at her from the floor, himself seemed transformed, as though tainted with malice. Her tears made the child's face blur, distort beyond recognition, and she had a brief moment when she saw only a stranger, a creature, and wished him harm. But she wiped her eyes, and his face again appeared, pale and attentive, his beautiful mouth always a little open, and she smiled at him, and it passed.

Spring ended, fell into summer. The year thickened, found a new pace. Anna realised she was living not in the expectation but the aftermath of love. The know-ledge was not startling – nothing, she began to suspect, would ever startle her again after the feeling of Orr's hands between her thighs, and their removal – but it settled in her with a precision, starting as a simple, unarticulated thought but quickly colonising her entire self, her expectations, her desire. She was young still, barely twenty-eight, and attractive. But her attention roamed little further than her child and her work, and she was struck herself by the lack of hunger for another man to replace Orr.

She decided to take Sam away for a month. The talk she had given at Barcelona at the end of the previous year had gone well – she was amused by the complicated satisfaction that Orr had left his mark on her speaking style also, as she became more laconic, more confident in pausing, reading the audience, finding a rhythm, a humour – and, when it was discovered she was writing her own poetry, she had been invited to return to Spain for a month-long residency, in order to devote some time to finishing her first collection of poems. Her mother offered to look after Sam, but she decided to take him with her.

She worked intently, daily, with a kind of hunger. She would get up early, before Sam woke, and write, and the poems quickly found a rhythm and shape she suspected they would not have fallen into in Ireland. After breakfast they would explore the city, and new poems surfaced from their wanderings, Anna finding herself looking through Sam's eyes, the everyday made once again strange, people and cars and windows and chairs compressed, or elevated, into colour and form and movement. When the collection was published more than one reviewer noted the fault line running through it: on one side, the force and excess and annulling of a love affair, and on the other, the remaking of a world in its aftermath, through the eyes of the resulting child.

One poem in the book seemed to stand alone. In a back street in the Gothic Quarter, Anna and Sam had witnessed the police drag a group of Africans out of a shop. One of them was carrying a child, not much older than Sam, and as he was manhandled towards the open doors of a van, he thrust the child into Anna's arms. She reached out for him immediately, instinctively, and stood frozen, staring at this small, black boy in her arms, his eyes fearless and trusting. A policeman sharply snatched the child from her and walked quickly away, beyond the van. She moved to follow him but was pushed back by another policeman, his finger raised in warning, ready for violence. She stood silently, watching them go, until the street was again empty, as though nothing had happened.

She returned again and again to the scene, her note-books bent on unravelling something she could not, at first, put her finger on. The aftermath felt like a betrayal, the empty street a lie. She was aware of her assumption of the men's crime: that the men being dragged out had done something wrong, and were therefore receiving punishment. What was taking place was a correction. It did not take her long to reassess this; even as she had held the child this had changed, the policemen within seconds passing from an impersonal force of justice into something sinister and disturbing. But her *initial sense*, in its immediacy, before the evaluation of what was actually before her, had assumed a guilt, and she was troubled afterwards at the ease with which this impulse came to her. She felt that she had not given herself to it, but that it had somehow claimed her; and that her *action* was not in believing in the guilt, but in refusing the belief, and that therefore her passive state, her underlying disposition, was embedded in a kind of hidden authoritarianism she had not been aware of. The question of race, and of otherness – the men being hauled away were black men – did not escape her.

The more troubling sense, however, to which she could not stop herself returning was the simple, dark thrill of being present when *something had happened*. That the violence, in all its brutality and despite her absolute refusal of it, and her unquestionable sympathy with the men and the child, had been energising, enlivening. For the briefest of moments, life had been condensed to a series of staccato bursts, vital, electric. The brutality quickly tainted the excitement, but some aftertaste remained, which filled her in spite of herself.

They returned to Belfast in the early summer. Anna walked into her house to find the back window smashed in, a half-brick lying on the floor. Fragments of glass lay on the worktop, on the tiles, glinting in the sunlight. The surfaces around the window were wet, presumably from rain, though it was not now raining. She picked up Sam suddenly and ran back to the car, locking him inside. She returned to the house, picking up the shaft of a brush that was sitting against the side wall.

As she stepped inside she recognised the foolishness of what she was doing, but went forward anyway, drawn towards whatever she would find, craving, to her own surprise, a confrontation. This appetite was new in her; there was a rawness of desire for some violence, a taste of blood in her mouth. She stepped into one room, then another, then climbed the stairs. By the time she reached the landing she knew there was no one there. She felt it. Nothing was out of place, everything was as it should be, the house composed and untouched, broken only at its skin. She checked the bedrooms, then walked to the window overlooking the garden at the back. It was early evening; the sun hung low in a pale sky. She stared out, and collected herself, and shuddered suddenly to think that the anonymous brick was a message, not simply an intrusion. Had she surprised a burglar, or found something missing, it would merely be a crime; she would merely be someone who had something worth taking. But there was no theft, no break-in. It did not feel random.

Orr came to her house the next day, to collect Sam. He had not seen the child in months, and had called Anna more often in the last week of their trip, evidently missing the boy. Orr's life had discovered an equilibrium of sorts, returning to the mission hall as pastor, but continuing to work on cars during the week, and the tangible physicality of the work had created a balance he realised he had for a long time been missing. An awkwardness, slight but evident, persisted in Orr's engagement with Anna, an embedded heaviness that referred, by never referring, to the love they had shared, and everything that had followed. Their interactions circled it but left it untouched; like pen marks scribbled all over a page except for one small, clean space, a palpable emptiness.

In the kitchen he saw the broken window, a piece of cardboard fixed to the frame. He nodded towards it – Orr's nods were questions – and Anna told him what she had returned home to find. Orr stared at it in silence, his face suddenly slack; as though, Anna thought, he had just discovered it himself.

What is it? Anna asked him.

Orr shook his head.

Do you know who did this?

He sat down in a chair at the small table. It might have been Philip, he said.

Philip had, step by slow step, turned his anger into a solid thing, a weapon. His control was remarkable, the level of restraint he exercised. He had become, at fifteen years old, Orr claimed, a craftsman of hatred, like one of those child chess masters who live the game, who see pieces moving in their sleep, the world a series of black and white squares. Orr unfolded a story to Anna, or a series of stories, one after the other, of the tiny abrogations of love Philip had managed in the previous eighteen months, small intrusions, scarcely perceptible, but building upon one another, like a series of paper cuts, a kind of domesticated cruelty, barely worthy of the word. The effect, nonetheless, was impressive. Philip had the measure of Orr's moral weakness, the exactitude of his failures, and exploited them with an uncanny calmness.

Orr recounted to Anna an old tale in which a metalsmith created a spear with such a fine point that it would pass through a person without them realising. The damage was done, the worst kind of damage, fatal damage, and yet the person carried on, oblivious, until everything inside ruptured, collapsed. Anna was conscious, as Orr played out his metaphor, that he felt it was himself who had received this wound, but she wondered if it wasn't rather Philip suffering, his hatred the weapon he was using on his father, but the real injury, as with the invisible spear, inflicted on himself.

The ways in which this hatred manifested, as Orr described them, were alternately subtle and blunt. On one occasion he reported to his school headmaster in tears, having found mocking graffiti in the locker room: PHILIP ORR FATHERS BASTARDS. The phrase made no sense, but the allusion was obvious, and Philip was in such a state that his father was called to the school. The headmaster, at Philip's insistence, took him to the locker to see the offending scrawl, and Orr saw in his son's face, hidden from the headmaster, a delight in his father's discomfort, and realised instantly that Philip had done it himself, had scraped his own locker, and created a sufficiently convincing performance to accompany it, to draw Orr in. And Orr, aware of how ludicrous an accusation would have been had he given voice to his suspicion, was rendered silent. Often the cuts were smaller, less histrionic: portraits of Sarah would move around the house, repositioned by Philip, usually incrementally, as though, said Orr, he was trying to make her follow him around. In all of this Philip made no direct complaint, no clear attack; it was a war of attrition, and Philip seemed utterly prepared to wage it without emotion or rage.

This calmness was described by Orr more or less exactly, but the internal cost to Philip is much harder to quantify; the paths of life inside himself he had to close down to enact such measured punishment. The surface may have been placid, but underneath Philip was surely molten. The energy he must have expended just keeping it in. His mother was dead, and the one avenue where he still might have received love he blocked off with impassive rigour. Orr had begun, after much prayer and self-examination, to push back. He had believed for such a long time that Philip would eventually relent, that he would run out of energy, or anger, or whatever other resources he was drawing on. But he had not. He had, if anything, grown in strength both internally and physically – as a fifteen-year-old boy he was almost six feet tall, taller already than Orr – and his animosity only seemed to burn with greater fierceness. And so Orr moved to address it. He had sought, he told Anna, biblical wisdom on the matter, but God, it seemed, had left him out in the cold. He picked his way blindly, and at every turn Philip matched him. He was obedient, so Orr could not fault him there, and his manners were impeccable, both in public and at home. One might have expected that some looseness would undo him when no one else was around, some discharge of temper; but his genius – Orr's word – was in maintaining it, like a method actor who finishes work on a film and forgets to return to his normal life. So Orr ended up driving at Philip's intent, and, by his own account, coming off

petty and weak. Philip denied everything, every awkwardly framed accusation, laughed them off, looking at
his father like he had gone mad. Do you know what you
are saying, father? he said on one occasion, as though
in imitation of a character in a Dickens novel, though
even this phraseology, as Orr admitted, was just normal
enough to make him uncertain if he was being mocked.
Anna assured him: he was.

But Orr's preparedness to take Philip on, to challenge
him, had shifted something, and in the last week, the
week before the window was smashed, Philip had asked
his father when his brother was coming home. Orr had
been cautious in reply – Philip's interest in his bastard
sibling had not registered in some time, barely at all
since Anna and Sam moved out – but he had read it as a
positive development, a sign that despite Philip's apparent frigidity, some hidden thawing was taking place.
However, in the subsequent days Philip had not followed
up his initial enquiry, and Orr now wondered if he had
not, rather, simply been working out the timescale for a
new assault, a widening of targets. Anna asked him why
she should be Philip's victim, especially now, since they
had had so few dealings in the previous year. And Orr
had no answer, just an instinct: By their fruits ye shall
know them, he said.

Anna sighed. Faith without works is dead, eh? was her
wry reply, and Orr could not resist a smile.

The hurling of a brick through a window was hardly
an insinuation that could be, without any evidence what-
soever, hurled back at the boy, but both Anna and Orr
agreed that they could not simply ignore the possibility,

and so they agreed that Orr would – for the first time in almost two years – bring his three boys to Anna's house, for a visit. They could not think of a pretext, but decided that only Philip would demand a pretext anyway; that the two younger children, although they may be surprised, would not complain. In this they were proved partially right: only Philip raised his eyebrows when Orr made the announcement over dinner later that evening, though in fact he said nothing, merely smiled, a hint of satisfaction passing across his face, of recognition. He did not ask why, he did not complain; Orr was unnerved by this, and called Anna to tell her. She dismissed his fears. Maybe he's not what you have made him out to be, she said. You have a propensity for stories, she said, with some satisfaction.

Anna had left the cardboard in place, putting off the glazier until after the visit of Orr and the boys; she felt manipulative, aware of the dark pleasure she was getting in anticipating Philip's reaction, of seeing his face, but could not relinquish it. When Anna opened the door only Orr and the younger two were initially visible; Philip lurked behind, detached. But when she stepped back and they made their way inside, Philip moved towards her with a smile, and hugged her as he entered. It was entirely unexpected, and she was uncertain of how to respond to this boy, this man-boy, and briefly hated herself, hated how much her body was still the property of Orr, of how her contraction at Philip's embrace was because of him. She moved into the embrace but too late, and she knew that Philip had sensed it, had felt the incompleteness of it. She felt shame immediately, her judgement already, against her own will, passed. She looked at Orr with an almost palpable anger as Philip walked away, and was still staring at him when she heard Philip's voice from the kitchen: What happened to your window?

Orr looked at her, and Anna felt that same contraction, felt something detach inside her, and she knew Orr had been right, and that Philip had thrown the brick, and was so utterly in control that he could walk straight to it, deliberately and fearlessly, to nod at it like a handyman assessing an unfortunate breakage. It was the lack of fear, she said later, that unnerved her. She did not feel herself to be in actual, physical danger; but some immeasurable unease now flickered at the edge of things, some refusal of peace. When you close your eyes you feel everything should go black, but it doesn't. Some light bleeds through.

When they followed him into the kitchen, Philip was poking at the cardboard, testing it. He turned and smiled at her.

It'll be fixed tomorrow, she said.

Oh, that's good, he replied, and took his finger away.

He sat down at the table, in the same seat Orr had been sitting in days previously, and Anna was struck by the likeness. The same fineness of line along his cheek, the intensity of look; though Orr's kindness, his almost physical approachability which she had long tried to assess (was it in the hold of his shoulders, the line of his mouth?), was perfectly absent from his son. It was astonishing to behold. She detested herself for thinking it, but it came without her permission, this wave of hatred, as though he had drawn it out of her. He was a crucible, the thought came, unbidden, for the opposite of everything she had loved in Orr. Christ and antichrist. All of this flooding her, almost wordless, as Philip stared, the half-smile, an almost imperceptible nod. Yes, he was saying, yes. It is what you think. And even more. Yes.

Anna's book was published at the end of the summer. The title was taken – stolen, wrote one reviewer, which amused Anna greatly – from Beckett. *If I Do Not Love You I Shall Not Love.* Poetry rarely created a stir, and this publication did nothing to change that. Still, Anna, at almost thirty years old, moved from academic anonymity into a small but revered space of creative community. She began to receive invites to events of all sorts: gallery openings, book launches, even political gatherings, and every few months would be persuaded to give a talk. At first she turned most of these invitations down, but shortly found herself – this is how she thought of it, as though it were something happening to her, rather than an action of her choosing – attending more and more, and making friendships with others on the fringes of the small Belfast scene, usually other solitaries, writers and artists, similarly sceptical of public profile but tied to the game through their careers, if that is the right word for an often unrewarded artistic commitment. One of these was an older man, in his mid-fifties, a painter called Patrick Curran. Curran taught occasionally at the art college but spent most of his time painting landscapes

in a small barn in the Antrim hills, attached like an
anchorhold to the side of his cottage. He threw paint
on thick, as often with a knife as with a brush, and,
like Cézanne had done with the hills around Provence,
created a significant and impressive body of work simply
by watching the light change in one place; for Curran,
Glenariff. The modern world of painting had passed him
by, he was aware, but somehow his very lack of fashion-
ability, his naïve commitment to painting in what was
still, more or less, an impressionist manner, albeit with
considerable skill, allowed him to carve out a career
freed from contemporary fascinations, and he was for
the most part respected by other artists. He was large,
with a face quick to smile, and a quietness in company
which belied a sharp wit and a rough, familiar kindness.
He was married to Edie, who taught at a small primary
school in Cushendall, the nearest sizeable town, less than
six miles from their home.

Curran took to Anna, her wryness, her quietness of
manner, the unforced control she seemed to have at a
platform while reading a poem or delivering a short
lecture, and he asked her to come to dinner at the cottage. They were at an art opening, a new group show at
which Curran had a couple of paintings, and they were
discussing *Molloy*, sharing an appreciation for Beckett's
tongue-in-cheek, boyish humour, his affection for the
puerile. They had met on a couple of occasions previously, though they had exchanged only a nod and and a
How are you, and she did not really know him when the
invitation was first made. He saw the hesitation in her
eyes, and recognised immediately, or so he later told her,

that she had been hurt by a man before and would not
be hurt again. He smiled – that broad, open smile – and
assured her that his wife would be there. Anna smiled
then too, relaxing, and accepted.

Alongside her friendship with Curran, a new relationship
had begun, surprisingly, to form with Philip. Following
the incident with the window, he at first seemed to
retreat into himself. His bravado, his finger on the cardboard, the sheer brazenness with which he owned Anna's
kitchen, seemed to be a high point from which he slowly
retreated. He still gave no inch to Orr, but the directness
of his attacks changed, subdued, and the front that Anna
feared was opening up on herself never materialised.
What did happen, eventually, was much more surprising,
to both Anna and Orr.

Within a couple of months of her return from
Barcelona, Anna's disquiet had all but disappeared, and
the routine had re-established itself without complication, Orr's attention for Sam continuing to grow and
soften. It was a period, Anna began to feel, of genuine
peace; a brief season, six months or so, of an almost
effortless contentment. Orr himself seemed, for reasons
Anna could not determine, to take a step back from
his own intensity. The simplicity of the happiness he
appeared to have discovered with Sam dismantled, or
at least tempered, his zeal, and it struck Anna that he
was again, over three years since they had first met, and
after a significant retreat into a harsh, solitary wilder-
ness from which she – and Sam – had been ruthlessly
excluded, more like the man she had captured on her

camera smilingly emerging from his tiny church. She was reluctant to dwell on this, and refused herself, or tried to refuse herself, the idea that a clearing was opening up into which they might once again move, the hurts of the recent years subsiding and love once more possible. Whatever stirred in her, whatever hopes were glowing below, breathing slowly, she made no move towards Orr; but the ease in their interaction created a genuine satisfaction, which had for a long time been missing. Into this ease stepped Philip.

He appeared at Anna's door at the end of the August. She opened to the rung bell and was taken aback to find him standing there, black T-shirt and jeans, his arms loosely tracing his sides. His hands, though still, appeared to be moving, twitching, though Anna was uncertain if perhaps she was imagining it.

I thought you might need your grass cut, he said.

Anna was briefly struck dumb. She stammered for an answer, nodding. Did your father send you?

He shook his head. No.

She felt she could not refuse him. She led him around the back and unlocked the shed where the mower and shears were kept.

She retreated to the house and waited on an attack, unaware of what it might look like, of what mix of kindness and cruelty it might be formed. Philip went about his business as he had promised. He mowed the lawn and tidied the garden, carrying the grass and hedge cuttings by hand in bags to the skips a quarter-mile away. Anna watched him from Sam's room, his young body moving into the work with the same strange grace she had seen in

his father. The severity of her previous reactions seemed
suddenly unfair, untrue even, and more than once she
walked away from the window, troubled by a combination of thoughts and yearnings to which she could not
give names.

As he left her house that first evening she invited him
in. He looked at his feet, and for the first time she had
ever seen, appeared uncertain of himself, almost shy.
Then he looked up at her and smiled – Orr's smile – and
she found herself catching her breath, exposed, as though
she had been caught naked.

Next time, he said, and walked away.

He came again, the following week. There was less
to do in the garden, only a week's growth, and he finished his work much earlier. The sun was dropping just
above the houses one street over, the shafts beginning to
pierce the gaps between them. The garden was bathed
in a warm glow, and Anna, looking from her kitchen
window, felt some corresponding warmth inside herself,
a peace beating through her, heartbeat by heartbeat.
Birds were returning to the trees for the night, their low
calls rising in volume. Anna pushed open the window
and called to him. Come and have a drink.

They stood in the kitchen, drinking Coke from
glasses, saying little. They had never been alone together,
like this, and the awareness crept up on Anna suddenly,
her mouth dry and awkward. Philip did not seem to
notice. He held himself differently, she thought as she
watched him, without the aloofness, the distance she
was used to. She talked to fill the gaps, though he did
not seem to feel unnerved or anxious. She talked about

how she loved the time of year, of the changing seasons, of the threat and promise of winter. He didn't say much, just nodded in a teenage way, smiled occasionally, rattled the ice against the glass when he had finished drinking.

I should go, he said finally, setting his glass in the sink. Thanks for the Coke.

Anna nodded as he opened the back door and stepped outside.

In the week that followed she returned again and again to their conversation, one-sided as it had been, poking at the edges, the corners, trying to uncover something that would reveal him, but there was nothing there. In any other context there would have been nothing to explore; he was just a kid helping with the gardening. But there was so much underlying their relationship that she could not let go of the need for a meaning, or rather a motive. The previous week she had not mentioned to Orr that he had visited. She was not sure why, but she had felt that whatever thawing, whatever engagement was occurring, it was between her and Philip. On the following Saturday, however, when Orr came to collect Sam, she told him. He hesitated before replying; she saw his body contract, saw him search for a rationale the way she herself had done. Before he even spoke she knew he had nothing to say, that he knew no more than she did, and that Philip's reaching out, if that was what it was, was separate from his father, distinct. She made Orr promise not to mention it to him; if Philip was moving in this direction, if this was the opening he needed to let go of his animosity and fear, then Anna would provide it. Orr was resistant, but

Anna held her ground, demanded from him his word, and, shaking his head, he gave it.

And so a tentative, unspecified pattern evolved; for the next couple of months it was still tied to Philip's work in the garden, but by November, when it was cold outside and the leaves and grass required less attention, a kind of camaraderie had established itself between them, even – Anna hesitated to use the word – a friendship. One week he turned up early, still in his school uniform. He was sitting on her front step, freezing, when she arrived home with Sam. She was struck by how young he looked in his blazer and tie, a kind of false armour, seeming to distance him from the perils of adult life, with which he was already far too familiar. He smiled immediately, and Sam rushed up to him, the affection they had created so early still evident.

I'm sorry, I know I'm not supposed to be here yet, he said, and Anna shook her head and told him it was okay, of course, and brought him inside. She made dinner. He told her he had had a fight with another boy in school, and had won the fight but it was not over, he had simply made more enemies, who would come for him when the time was right.

Are you scared? she asked him.

Scared? No, he answered flatly.

Why are you telling me? she asked.

He shrugged.

The following week she handed him a key. He stared at it, then at her.

You can come and go as you please, she said.

He held the key in his flat palm, as though weighing it. She waited for him to say something, and it seemed he was about to, but he remained silent.

Okay? she said, eventually, unnerved by his reticence. His face relaxed, the tautness fell away, and he smiled. Or, more truthfully, Anna felt, he tried to smile. I've thought often about this moment, this tiny window of possibility when something was given to Philip and he didn't know how to react. Can you imagine what went on within him as he stood there, contemplating his small victory, the turning of his enemy into his friend? How fucking Christlike, what a gift he must have had. But did he realise, even for a moment, the price he was paying? Did the reality of his inability to *win* descend upon him, the utter impossibility of it? Did he feel any dread at all, the sickening sense that he had, in rewriting all the rules to his advantage, rendered the game a joke? All his hatred suddenly a useless skill, like a man who spends years mastering the piano only to lose the feeling in his hands?

Perhaps I am being unfair. I am sorry. God knows I make up my own stories too.

As Philip entered her life, so too did Curran. The solitary Anna found herself opening up, connections forming that were as unanticipated as they were joyful. She drove up to Curran's house often, usually in the late afternoon, and would sit in his gallery as he worked, working herself on poems and articles, or sometimes just watching him paint. His cottage sat high in the glen, on the slope running down from the Lurig ridge. A large window overlooked the land spreading wide and low towards the sea at Waterfoot. A number of canvases stood on easels before the window and around the sides, always, it seemed, half completed, patches of greens and blues and greys echoing the landscape outside. He showed her what he was trying to do, the combination of rough, almost geometric blocks of earth tones interrupted by fine lines of much stronger, visceral colour, reds and yellows and blues, so fine sometimes as to be virtually invisible, but which deftly broke the regimentation, so that the painting seemed both tightly structured and yet free. I began to see nature a little late, he quoted Cézanne's letter to Zola, and Anna nodded, amused and impressed.

Curran roamed in conversation, a natural essayist, moving from the sublime to the mundane without a comma. How difficult it is to see what is in front of you, he said, and how strangely radical a commitment. He was talking of Cézanne. Curran was disdainful of the contemporary fascination with photorealism, seeing it as a kind of psychological naïvety, the belief that what you see is what there is. Reality, the Impressionists taught over a century ago, is unsteady, broken, elliptical, he said. Excess. There is more truth in one of Manet's discarded roses than in most galleries in London today, he complained. After a time Anna began to respond, to talk of her poetry, her frustration at finding herself always coming up short, and then her slow embrace of this failure, her growing sense that mastery was not the point, that if she could just aim her words in the right direction she would have succeeded, or perhaps failed in a useful way. Curran smiling. Failed in a useful way, he echoed. Put that on my gravestone.

They ate lamb stew and drank wine. Edie was sometimes there, sometimes not. Occasionally Sam would
be left with Anna's mother, and Anna would stay over,
drinking Scotch in front of the open fire, climbing late
into the small bed in the spare room.

Everything is changing, Curran told her one night, out
of nowhere, as though continuing a conversation he had
been having in his head. I'm leaving the university. Do
you know they are starting a new course at the art college
next year? Gaming. It's actually War Gaming. The idea
is to design simulations which come closer and closer
to real-world conflict situations. Do you know who is
paying for the course? The British Army. Apparently the
Americans have been at it for years. There are forty-five
undergraduate courses being offered next year, he told
her. Do you know how many are not being part-funded
by a commercial sponsor? Two, he said. And they're both
mine. They tried to sell Nineteenth Century to Shell.
Oil Painting. They were going to call it, no word of a
lie, Oil Painting.

Anna recalled the conversation less for Curran's revelation than for her own. When he had finished talking
about his job, about the uncertainty of his future, she told
him about Orr, about their affair, about Sarah's death,
about living now between fragile expectations, love's
inevitable unravelling. She had not intended to pour herself out like this. But Curran's candour, his lack of poise,
drew an intimacy that surprised even herself, and she
spoke – for the first time, she realised – with frankness
and honesty about the past years, and found in it a relief
she had not expected. When she finally went to bed,

she lay staring at the ceiling, her head spinning from a combination of the whisky and the feeling of *having been seen*, a kind of recognition she had rarely before experienced. It was not like Orr, she considered, deliberately; with Orr she felt like she was dissolving, like the edge of her body was blurring into the world, the lines between everything obscured and redundant. With Curran she felt almost the opposite, a mutual acuity, as though she were solidifying, finding and testing the limits of herself and finding that they worked, that they held her together, and the person that moved around inside them was acceptable, knowable.

She awoke the next morning to sunlight streaming through the small window above her bed, throwing a stark brightness on the dresser at the far end of the little room, where there was a number of small moulded figures, animals and people, who appeared ablaze. She lay there watching the light move incrementally along the surface, sliver by sliver, until it dripped off them one by one, moved on to find new objects to alight on, and after twenty minutes they were all in shadow. She chased the image into a poem; the sense of being one of those figures, briefly in the sunlight, glowing, but utterly helpless to move where the light moved. I can still almost feel the light sliding off, the spot on the skin where, just a second before, what had been heat was now darkness.

These visits – this visit, even, perhaps – changed Anna. She found with Curran a way to be vulnerable. Her autonomy, her self-sufficiency was contained, softened. Curran, in his mannered love of the creative process, and the warmth and width of his humour, drew Anna out of herself, and she began sending him snippets of poems, phrases and stanzas as yet unmoored. He helped anchor them, helped her tease out a direction, a line around which she could unravel an idea. If the line was strong enough – a metaphor he had built into his own process as a painter – one could throw different images, different weights and measures around it and the poem would gain an energy, a momentum. It would, he said, spin. If there was no line it would just career off, lurch from verse to verse, all energy and no control. It may have life, but it would totter and sway like a drunk.

In the next few months she worked and worked at the poems, which were eventually published as her second collection. Curran made suggestions, criticisms, threw praise where he felt praise was warranted, and pushed her to reconsider images, to dig further into an earthiness, a materiality of words. Anna grew in confidence, and began to push back against some of his suggestions, and this conviction, the *rightness* with which she both embraced his judgement and resisted it, gave the poems a personality that they had, she realised, been missing. She found a way to not fear the emotion the poem could create, to commit herself to feeling, despite the proximity to sentimentality that she was desperate to avoid. By the time she was finished with them, these new poems had a boldness that her work had not had before. By then, of course, she had other things on her mind.

·

By the end of the year Philip was a regular visitor. In the first few weeks after she gave him a key, he continued to visit weekly, would spend an hour or so in the garden, cleaning and tidying. Winter was already beginning to wreak its steady destruction; he merely had to pick up after it. He would then come inside, eat dinner, play with Sam – now almost three years old, throwing words around with gleeful curiosity – and talk to Anna. His friendship with Sam, the genuine affection they had for one another, continued to erode Anna's fear, and a closeness soon developed between them which mirrored that growing between her and Curran. In one sense at least Curran cleared the way for Philip; his influence, the openness he had created in her towards her own vulnerability, allowed her a similar openness to Philip.

They began to share their lives. Anna confided in the boy, began to talk to him about her poetry, about her friendship with Curran, about his painting. About the joy of discovering, at thirty years old, that one could still find something new, alive, meaningful. She did not talk about Orr; a line seemed drawn around him as a subject, a barrier erected. But it had faded sufficiently within a few months so as to barely cross her mind, and where once she had been constantly aware of what she was avoiding, by early in the new year they had so much else to talk about, so many other connections, personal to each other, that Orr was largely unconsidered. This freedom cannot have been the same for Philip. He returned home every day to his father, and whilst a truce of sorts had been established between them, his anger and sense of betrayal had not diminished. He was sixteen years old, somewhere between a boy and a man. He sounded like a teenager, the twisted, playful phraseology, the voice still finding its timbre; but something else, a ferocity that he could never push down quite far enough, betrayed him as an adult.

Sam turned three in January. Anna held a party for the family, inviting Orr and his sons, and her mother. Just a year before, Anna could not have imagined this gathering taking place. Orr drove the boys across town on the first Saturday of the new year, a few days after Sam's birthday. It was too cold to play outside, but she had covered a table in food, sweets and crisps, and they ate and joked, and Sam blew out the candles on the cake. Afterwards the boys helped him set up the train set his father had bought him, Philip coaxing laughter from the child by pretending to put the pieces in the wrong order. Anna and Orr and her mother stayed in the kitchen. Anna put on another pot of tea. She watched Orr standing in the doorway, glancing around repeatedly at the scene in the living room.

Why do you keep looking? Anna asked him.

He shook his head. He looked at her mother, as though weighing up whether he could speak.

Spit it out, Anna said. She was surprised at her defensiveness, her need to stand in Philip's corner; it had sneaked up unannounced. Orr stared at her. Anna remembered the way he used to stare at her, and found it astonishing how much was still left. For a moment she wished her mother were someplace else.

Just be careful, Orr said, his voice barely audible.

Is that a warning? Anna asked him.

He glanced around again, and Anna looked past him to see Philip watching them, his face unreadable.

And then Philip smiled at her, and looked back at Sam, made a joke, and Orr turned to Anna, and said flatly, Yes. Yes it is.

Something shifted after this, Anna believed. Not in her, but in Orr. She could not work out exactly what it was. She thought that he felt backed into a corner, ganged up on; that he had sensed a danger and come out fighting. Cause and effect are so complicatedly positioned; one so easily becomes the other. Anna afterwards never quite forgave herself for this. In reading Orr this way, she reacted all the more strongly against him, moving further and further into Philip's camp, distancing herself from Orr, trying to force him to retreat.

What Orr was supposed to have done, of course, was relayed to her largely by Philip himself. His visits became weighed down with accusations, a grammar of violation. He knew Anna by now. Despite her never talking directly about Orr, about their relationship, Philip had an extraordinary skill of carefully unpicking a person's weakness, of paying attention as much to what they didn't say as to what they did. He had an ear for the repressed, the skilfully avoided. And he had that rare absence of compassion, a preparedness to use whatever he could get his hands on for his own ends. And so the subtle, pointed comments, the references to Orr's holiness, his authority, his failure to consider sufficiently the pain of others. He was careful never to accuse Orr of anything in which Anna herself might be implicated.

Accuse, in fact, is too strong a word. Anna said later, looking back with regret, that when he left there was never a clear picture in her head of what Orr was alleged to have done, but rather an atmosphere, a kind of barbed, muted anger which had been created and in which she found herself a participant.

Orr drifted further and further, the friendship between him and Anna – for a while so easy again – now slowly, clumsily unwound. They still saw each other twice a week, but rather than an interaction Sam was simply passed between them, like a baton. Sometimes she didn't get out of the car when she dropped him off. Anna said later she didn't notice the extent to which the gap between them was widening. There was no deliberation, no decision. It happened under the surface and rose upward; the crack appeared, the chasm, only at the end. Anna's friendship with Curran, growing in scope and affection, tempered, disguised even, the extent of the other breakages.

It was March when everything turned. Or April, I suppose. In March the seeds were sown. Around the middle of the month, on a Thursday night, Philip appeared at the door. It was shortly after ten o'clock. Anna peered through the window first, surprised at being disturbed so late. She gasped to see Philip's face, bloody and badly bruised, with a gash on his left cheek, still open. He was holding it shut with his T-shirt. His shirt was unbuttoned, his chest also showing wounds, pale patches of violence. Anna brought him inside, her heart racing. Philip himself seemed unperturbed, almost unnaturally calm.

What happened? she asked him.

I told you they would wait for the right time, he replied.

But this, she said. For God's sake.

He sat at the kitchen table as she attended to the immediate wounds. You have to go to the hospital, she said.

He shook his head. No.

You have to, Philip, she said. Look at you.

You can fix me, he said.

Jesus, no I can't. He nodded, closed his eyes.

It doesn't hurt, he said.

Whether it was the shock, or the necessity of the moment, Anna found herself moving mechanically, cleaning the wound on his cheek, applying iodine, gently wiping off the blood on the more minor scratches. His chest was a collection of changing colours, blues and reds. The image came to her of Curran's paintings.

Does your father know? she asked him.

He shook his head.

Your cheek will scar, she said, after she had finished.

His eyes were still closed. He had barely flinched, even as the stinging fluid burned the bacteria from his cuts. He was indifferent, a teenage Buddhist. Only pain, no suffering.

Whatever, he said.

She made up a bed for him on the sofa. When she left him he thanked her. She lay awake in her bed, picturing his chest, his broken skin. *Whatever.* She could not separate him, she found to her surprise, from his father. She closed her eyes but the images repeated over and

over, first the boy, then the man, Orr's lips on her body
and her hands on the boy's, and she shuddered awake,
sweating.

In the morning she rose early. He was still asleep,
on his back, the way his father slept. His breathing was
quiet, calm. The plasters on his cheek had stained red,
but seemed to have worked to hold the cut closed. She
made tea and sat in the kitchen, staring out the window.
It was spring, trees returning to bud. Birds sang. The
traffic rose slowly, the rumble of the city imperceptibly
growing. Philip appeared in the doorway. They looked
at each other. She shook her head, and – unable to do
anything else – smiled. He sat across from her and she
poured him tea.

Now what? she said.

Now what what? He smiled, then winced, raising his
hand to his damaged face.

No smiling for you, she said.

She reached across towards him, towards his face. He
moved back, instinctively. I'm not going to hurt you,
she said. He stared at her, then let her touch him. She
appraised the plasters. It's working. But I still think you
should go to the hospital.

He shook his head. I'm not going to the hospital.

She got up, began to tidy the kitchen. I have to go to
work. She heard a door open upstairs. Sam's up.

Can I stay here today? Philip asked.

Don't you have school? she replied. He looked at her.
Yes, okay, you can stay, she said.

You can leave Sam if you like, he nodded, as Sam
appeared in the doorway.

Anna recalled the moment with clarity, looking at the two boys, the sunlight in strips blinding Sam as he stared at them both, raising his arm to cover his face. She returned to this particular moment over and over again, as though there were something in it she should have seen, some augur, a sign of what was to come. But there wasn't, or if there was, she didn't see it. It was just three people in a kitchen, in the aftermath of an unknown act of violence, looking at each other, the sunlight making them squint, grimace, and rendering each of them, in its harshness, difficult to apprehend.

She didn't leave Sam with Philip that day, but brought him to her mother's, as usual; still, the offer had been made, and in it she felt an opportunity to ease some of the pressure on her mother, who had continued to be quietly, passively supportive, taking the boy as often as was needed. The following week she asked Philip if he would look after Sam on Friday night. He had visited her most evenings already. His face was healing, though slowly, and she felt he was enjoying her role as his nurse. She had been invited to an opening with Curran. Philip agreed without hesitation. Sam was thrilled, and talked incessantly of what they would do, the games they would play, the fun they would have.

When she returned home, around eleven, Philip was playing on his phone. He glanced up as she walked in, barely removing his attention from the screen.

He's asleep, he said.

Anna went upstairs, looked in on him, sleeping soundly. She changed out of her evening dress, put on a sweatshirt. She went back downstairs and found Philip in the kitchen, making tea.

Decaf, right? he said.

Thanks, she said, and sat down.

How was it? he asked.

She smiled and took the mug he held out. It was good. How was your night?

Philip smiled. It was good too. He sat down opposite her.

Are you not having a cup?

He shook his head.

You can stay here tonight, she said. He looked at her. If you want. On the couch. I'll get you blankets.

He nodded. She was a little drunk. She reached across the table, touched his cheek. She moved her thumb over the tiny crust of blood along the wound, where the line held.

It doesn't hurt, no, he said.

How did you know I was going to ask that? she smiled.

You always want to know that, he said.

She was briefly silent, and then said, You remind me of your father.

She was not sure, retrospectively, whether she was trying to provoke a reaction, or whether her slight intoxication had simply freed her to say something she had been so actively hiding before. She agonised over it at length, wondered at that part of her that must have wanted to punish him. She knew that he would not have liked the comparison. He flinched as she said it, but managed not to draw himself away. Indeed, she thought, she almost felt him move closer, though again she could not be sure whether this was a physical movement or a shift taking place inside her, the alcohol mixed with the giddy thrill of having said the wrong thing and got away with it. The moment lasted, she thought, two, three seconds and then she realised, as though suddenly, where she was, and she pulled her hand back, too fast perhaps, her head spinning.

She did not remember getting Philip the blankets for the sofa, nor going to bed herself. She dreamed that she awoke in the middle of the night and he was standing in her doorway, framed by light from behind, his body lithe, animal.

And so here we are.

Orr called Anna early the following week. They fought on the phone, about Philip again, Orr again warning her that she was walking a dangerous path. There was too much of the Bible in his language for her to listen. She heard only a petty rival, a jealous god. She accused him then, words stored up and sharpened, and hung up the phone alive with the tingle of self-righteousness. She walked around the rest of the day replaying the conversation, augmenting her arguments with further observations, nodding inwardly, her convictions strengthened. She wondered she had not done it sooner. There was a slight tremble in her hands. Her blood seemed to run faster. Too much blood, too little space.

*

Two weeks later Anna again left Sam with Philip. This time she was at a concert, a festival of Spanish music organised by the music department of the university, at which she'd been asked to read some poems from her time in Barcelona. Her second collection was due to be published a couple of months later. She left hurriedly, dishevelled. Philip himself seemed distracted, watching her without speaking. His face was largely healed, save the one large scar on his cheek, which remained, greedily drawing attention from his other features. You know where everything is, she said, leaving, without waiting for his response.

They usually played together, but now Philip switched on the television and they sat in front of it. Anna rarely allowed Sam to watch, so it was still a pleasure, an almost illicit joy. He sat on the floor, staring up, unmoving. After some time, perhaps an hour, he looked around to find that Philip was not in the room. He got up, walked around the house, but could not find him. He climbed the stairs, and heard a noise from his mother's room.

At first Philip did not see him and Sam stood silently, staring. Philip turned around, suddenly aware he was being watched. The look on his face was of neither surprise nor shame; he glared with impatience.

What are you doing? Sam asked.

Get on to the bed, Sam.

Why?

Just do it.

Are we going to play a game?

Philip paused, nodded. A game, yes.

Sam climbed on to the bed. He was excited, thrilled to be with his brother.

Close your eyes, Philip said.

A hesitation on Sam's part, but he closes his eyes.

Whatever happens, you keep your eyes closed, right? That's the game.

Sam squeezes his eyes shut tighter. Okay, he says.

For a moment nothing happens. Outside, the distant drone of a lawnmower. The room itself is silent.

Suddenly, the sharpest pain across his cheek. The door slams. He opens his eyes and tries to look down at where his cheek is but can see nothing, he can only feel, a stinging, hot. Pain spreads across his face. Philip has gone.

I raise my hand to my cheek and take it away. There is blood all over it.

This is my first memory.

And God said, Let there be light: and there was light. And God saw the light, that it was good: and God divided the light from the darkness . . . And the evening and the morning were the first day.

The light shineth in darkness; and the darkness comprehended it not.

IV

A new Caravaggio. I say new. You know that I have worked at the Met for almost fifteen years? Okay. I mean, someone found it, the C, in a basement in some tiny village outside Rome, wrapped in what could be described as swaddling bands (I know). Amazing that these things still happen. The Met outmuscled the Prado and bought it. Balthasar and I were allocating. All song and dance. With these bigger events – even with the excitement about working them – there was always pressure on the rota. In the end, regardless of all the moving around and overtime, we were still short of guards. For old times' sake? he asked me. You know, Sam, it might do you no harm, remembering what it's like to be one of the little people.

So I end up, for a week, on the floor. I'd no interest in working the new piece – too many people – but I was happy enough, truth be told, to take Rubens-to-Vermeer. Six galleries. I knew every painting intimately, better than any of the other guards. I was on the floor for ten years before I moved upstairs, and – not to blow my own trumpet – they didn't promote me for no reason.

There was a skill, too. It looked simple, but there was more to it than standing around, making sure punters didn't get too close to the works, didn't stick their fingers where they shouldn't. When done right it was about a tone, a freedom. I was not blind to the fact that most of the visitors were not poor, that a line still existed that many people were unwilling or unable to cross. I lived still on the fringe of Bushwick, in a fourth-floor walk-up. My neighbours in the building were mostly working-class immigrants from Puerto Rico and the Dominican Republic, none of whom, I suspected, had ever set foot in the Met. Still, at least the space existed, the possibility, and if it didn't quite constitute democracy it came closer than a lot else in New York.

On the first day, as suspected, the Caravaggio drew the crowds and left the upper galleries quiet. I recalled when I had first started in the job, marking the days by measures of noise. In the downstairs galleries, among the mummies and Renaissance statues, a hubbub always arose, friendly chatter punctuated by laughter, easy banter; the phonetics of fifty languages floating in the air, snatches to be caught and tasted. But upstairs, among the paintings, there was silence, a hushed reverence. People dropped their voices to whispers, became intimate with one another, leaned in close to share thoughts. Thousands of times I watched visitors stop on their own before a painting, moved in a way they had not expected; for some, tears came. I remembered one man in his eighties who had come for a week and wept every day in front of Rembrandt's portrait of Gerard de Lairesse.

De Lairesse suffered from congenital syphilis and eventually went blind, and in Rembrandt's painting the disease is already ravaging his face, his features swollen. Rembrandt refuses to hide it, and it gives the painting an astonishing frankness, a brutal, compassionate honesty.

I was always intrigued by those visitors who were prone to be so touched. I would look for them as they entered the rooms I was attending. It was an art in itself; I slowly developed a sense, began to identify something in the way they moved, or looked, that I couldn't quite articulate, but which became increasingly accurate. It was not common, of course, this excessive reaction; but there were times I felt it coming as soon as the person even entered the room. I did not share this with anyone, not even my closest colleagues, aware of how it would have sounded. I had forgotten this sense over the years, away from the galleries, but I returned to it again, moving from room to room, watching people watching paintings.

The next morning my head rang, a tinny hollow echo I couldn't shake out. After work I'd gone with a few people for drinks at a tiny bar on Lexington. I didn't do this often, but it was Marcela's birthday, one of the few colleagues I counted as a friend. We started the job within a few months of one another, and quickly discovered a shared, private, almost embarrassed love of the work. We would leave the Met some evenings and head straight for the Whitney, or across to the Guggenheim, thirsty for more. There was nothing sexual in these jaunts, no demands extended beyond simple presence simply shared. She was new to the city, to the country, straight from Caracas, and whatever quantity of intimacy we both required, neither too much nor too little, we stumbled into easily. She was vibrant, generous; she told stories as though they would go out of date, witty and relentless. I loved these both for themselves and for the freedom they allowed me to simply listen, to offer my participation in the form of silence. Wise men speak only when they have something to say, etc. We wined it up and by midnight I was, as my mother would say, lit.

It had been so long since I had been hungover at work, I had forgotten how miserable it was. At break I threw down two cups of coffee and a pint of water. The floor a bit much for you? Balthasar joked.

At midday the galleries were still quiet. I moved slowly, appreciative of the peace. I was thinking – true story – of my mother, and resolved to call her. I had been lax of late. I walked through towards the Vermeers, the images forming in my mind before I even reached the paintings, the droplets of white, the paint transformed, catalysed into light. I walked towards my favourite, the *Young Woman with a Water Pitcher*.

I stopped at the entrance to the gallery. Someone was already standing in front of the painting, staring closely, moving his face around it, meerkat-like. It was an awkward, unusual movement. I had seen it before – there are no ways to look at a painting, I suspect, that I haven't witnessed – and yet something this time stopped me short, intrigued me. I watched him from twenty feet away, marked his clothing, the jacket cut well and fitted, the polished shoes, his hands clasped behind his back. He took a step back from the painting, a final pause to take it in as a whole, to recompose the pieces. As he moved off to the left, to the next painting, I saw it, the scar, and felt my throat constrict, my body knowing before the rest of me. Philip.

I moved swiftly, noiselessly backward, almost bumping into an old Chinese couple. I kept moving (get out of eyesight), then turned and walked straight through the galleries to the staff stairway. I punched the buttons and pushed through and walked, half ran, down the stairs into a dim corridor. I leaned against the wall, catching my breath. My hand instinctively went to my own face, and I consciously (self-consciously) pulled it back down again. How many years? I started counting, as though the discipline would help. Thirty-five. A smile caught up with me. I shook my head. It wasn't really Philip. How could it have been? Philip is dead. Thousands of people every day, millions every year, sooner or later someone was bound to look like my brother. Half-brother. I put a hand to my chest and felt my heart through my shirt, still beating, mocking me.

I started to walk back up the stairs, but quickly felt my throat again, the fear tight again, and stopped where I was. I tried to replay what just happened – as a child, my first therapist told me to do this with the original incident (incident!) when I had nightmares, a pretty stupid idea I thought even then – but each time he turned to the left, the scar ended everything, blurred the picture, cauterised the whole scene. I couldn't actually see his face, I realised. I hadn't seen him, I had seen only the scar. But I had seen scars before, and not reacted, not run. Jesus.

After five minutes of prevaricating I retreated to the staff room. I found Balthasar where I expected.

You are not in the right place, he said.

I am not well.

You are hungover.

I am going to throw up.

Avoid the Hogarths, he nodded.

Can you take over?

Go home, he said.

I walked quickly downtown, street followed by avenue, L-ing a diagonal distance, putting as much as I could between myself and the museum. I was going nowhere in particular, just away from where I'd been. He'd been. In thirty minutes I crossed the new footbridge into Queens, and began to slow down, the tension dissipating. I kept walking, past the cemeteries at New Calvary and Mount Zion, and finally hit Flushing. On Stanhope Street there was a kid's birthday party. Latin music pumping, helium-filled pink Disney balloons tied to the railings. The screams of the children, their boisterous playfulness, returned something to me, at least briefly. I walked up the four flights of stairs to my apartment a few minutes later with something approaching calm.

Are you not at work? Orr asked me, before I even closed the door. He was listening to music coming from a small speaker opposite him, as though it were his audience, or he its. I recognised Arvo Pärt's *In Principio*. I introduced my father to Pärt, when he first moved in with me. I had not expected him to like it, but he had taken to Pärt, and Tavener, and Górecki, immediately, and I experienced both a satisfaction and a theft, as though in the act of sharing I had had something taken away.

I'm not feeling well, I told him, and he looked at me as though he could see. I had to remind myself that he couldn't. It is a strange thing, this *presence* of my father.

There are none so blind as those who will not see. He ran the line off as a routine, whenever someone asked him about his eyes, or even if they didn't. Making light. He shuffled around Bushwick with his white stick, negotiating crossings with the help of passers-by, many of them Puerto Rican or Dominican, amused by him and his Irish accent, his endless stories. They were generous to him, and he to them, in his way, he thought, though he was less certain of himself than he had once been.

The area had changed from when he first arrived, almost ten years before. Gentrification had begun to parody itself; bars and cafés competed with their &s, their craft beers and artisanal baking. The little food stalls that once dotted the streets, offering *pinchos*, *empanadas*, *arepas*, were largely gone, as the people who frequented them moved away. Orr still visited daily the few remaining, including one run by a man he called Guest, a mispronunciation of his real name that was never corrected. Guest was at least as old as Orr, and had a voice low and kind, moving easily back and forth from Spanish to English. He wore clothes in the old Cuban style, *guayabera* shirts and a battered fedora. He changed the hat-band every few days: if my father guessed the colour correctly he got his lunch for free. Guest often told him he was right even when he wasn't.

At the weekends he was accompanied at the stall by his grandchildren, who also befriended Orr in their irreverent, easy manner, teasing and gently mocking him as he reeled off his tall tales. Orr had never felt so at home.

And how we got here? I had been in New York for almost ten years myself when my father arrived to live with me. At eighteen I left school. My mother secured me an invitation from one of her academic friends teaching at a small college in upstate New York, and so I visited America for the first time. The arrangement was simple: I would work in the college gardens for the summer, tending the lawns and hedges and flowerbeds on the small campus, and they would give me room and board. The invitation was, I suppose, an intervention on my mother's part. She worried about my listlessness, my frustration with life in Belfast, and felt that a few months away might help me find a path to follow, or at least break through what she saw as my languid hesitation about the future. I packed a bag, a few changes of clothes, a couple of Russian novels (the magnanimity of youth!) I felt would last me the break, and winged it across the ocean.

Anna saw listlessness, but it was something else. I was a marked child. My face wore a scar that I could forget for minutes, occasionally hours; but the memory would return, almost like the pain itself, and I would retreat back inside, chasing myself inwards, as though trying to bury something in my own body. I longed not to be seen.

Doctors did what they could, and with skin grafts and time the scar had faded. Still, it was impossible not to notice, and I had never in all the years since it happened met a single person whose eyes did not move there, find it immediately. It was a focal point; even when someone was not looking at it, they were, I knew, forcing themselves to look elsewhere. It was a gravitation, a black hole (my black hole!) which one gave in to or resisted. Unignorable me.

If this was it, the full measure, I might perhaps have found a different engagement, even an ownership. But the scar was only the method. Philip's deliberation, his preparedness, settled in me as my own, personal gospel. Philip, slicing his own face first: a test, refusing the hospital, making sure that Anna could repair it, that the damage done would be severe but not fatal. A precision that could barely be contemplated, and yet would never leave. And all for me. A gift. Reparation.

My first summer in Troy was perfect. It sounds excessive, I know: but really, I had never before experienced the freedom of working by myself all day, achieving something – creating beauty, coaxing nature into form – and getting up the next morning to do it all again. I stayed in a room in the college dorms, which were largely empty – only a handful of other students, also working manual jobs through the summer – and would wake in the morning without having to set an alarm, the birds chorusing outside my window. I did not often have to deal with people, and had whole afternoons to lose myself in, the rhythms of my body a new abandonment.

I made a friend. Oki was a couple of years older, from Ghana. He was studying chemistry, and had taken the job of looking after the labs over the summer. He was staying in the dorms too, and I ran into him for the first time in the shared bathrooms. Nice scar, was his opening comment, before turning his bare back to me and showing a gash of his own, running down half the length of his otherwise perfectly smooth body. I appreciated the directness of his observation, his apparent fearlessness. I began to look forward to returning in the evenings, began even, to my own surprise, to linger longer in the showers, hoping Oki would appear. Two or three times I woke in the middle of the night, startled awake by my finger running down the length of Oki's scar, my finger on Oki's skin. It took me a moment to come around, to realise I had been dreaming.

At the end of the summer, the college offered me a job. They were delighted with my work; in fairness, I was good at it. To bypass visa difficulties, they suggested I take a course at the college; they would allow me to study for free, and give me a stipend on top. I accepted on the spot. And lo, the mother rejoices.

I chose to study the history of art. It was an intuitive decision, immediate. I had grown up the child of a poet, whose best friend – now lover, we'll come to that – was a painter. Their choices, their refusal to accept the customary way to assign value, had not turned me into an artist myself, but it had created in me a hierarchy of value, and I felt different from other people my age. As a child I was fascinated by Curran's paintings. My mother often brought me with her on visits at the weekend, and Curran and I would paint together in his studio, canvases side by side in front of the huge windows above

the glens. Curran helped me mix paint, taught me how
to hold a brush, when and where to apply pressure, to
release. I loved to hear him describe me as a natural, and
loved Anna's reactions, dramatic and exaggerated as I
knew they were even then, to my presenting her with a
finished piece. For a while our living room at home was
like a gallery, and as many of the paintings hung around
the walls were mine as Curran's. This interest had run
its course by the time I was thirteen. I made my mother
take down my childish paintings, petulant and sulky as
I was, learning embarrassment with them as I was learning to be embarrassed with myself, a grammar of shame
colonising everything.

My studies opened up again in me, however, that earlier
thrill, that sense of discovery. The precision of the men
and women who for thousands of years had carved and
scraped and daubed at nature, reducing a piece of wood
or stone to a person or an animal in a way that somehow
resulted in an addition, an increase; it began to pulse in
me. Everything, indiscriminate, grabbed my attention:
those little wooden Pharaonic figurines, like children's
toys, workmen carrying baskets on their heads, filled
with small carved loaves like stretched communion
wafers; the Byzantine busts from Constantinople, all their
noses broken off, as though the people they remembered
had been themselves relentless brawlers; the dark, almost
black, bronze sculptures from the early Renaissance in
Italy, set off with a louche gold gilding that made me
think of crass hotels. Paintings too. El Greco's figures,
stretched and haunted, their eyes heavy and knowing, I

felt were almost shaking their heads at me. I discovered
Rubens, the sensualist, his plump people full of life and
sex and fat, so much more fleshy than his cautious con-
temporaries. It all made an impression, sank into me, and
I even began, tentatively, to sketch for myself, albeit in
the privacy of my dorm room.

My friendship with Oki continued, grew easily. He
was boisterous, large-hearted. His demands were a form
of generosity, such was the freedom he carried in himself,
which could transform the energy of a room he entered.
We went to parties together, met girls, drank – standard
college fare – and I watched Oki move from person to
person, group to group, with a looseness, an abandon
unconcerned of the expectations or opinions of others.
I could never manage this ease, much as I envied it,
and Oki was abundant enough unto himself not to be
troubled by my awkwardness.

During my first semester Anna came to visit. I hadn't
returned home before my studies began, had continued
the sparse, simple life I had lived during the summer, so
Anna filled a couple of duffels with the clothes and books
I'd left behind and brought them to me. She stayed with
her friend who had secured me the gardening job. Even
in the sultrier years of my teenage angst, my mother and
I had maintained an affection, a humour, fuelled in part
at least by our own solitariness, our sense of belonging to
no one except each other. So it was easy to return to the
routine of eating together in the evenings, trying out the
limited restaurants of Troy, accompanied occasionally by
Anna's friend or Oki.

My mother and Oki liked each other immediately. He's something else, she said to me, after the first time they met.

What do you mean? I asked her.

That swagger, she said. His feet barely touch the ground.

I laughed.

I'm sure the girls line up, she said. He reminds me of your father.

Anna had rarely mentioned Orr in years. She had had a couple of relationships as I grew up, though never anything serious. A handful of men at various stages passed tangentially through my life, barely registering. She did not need them, I suspect. Anna had found in Curran (another married man, Mr Freud?) the confidant she wanted, and sex was bracketed off into another territory, a zone for visiting but not setting up camp. As a teenager, desire growing in me as a forced, unwelcome appetite, I followed her in developing a capacity for keeping it at a remove, turning it from a need to a choice.

It felt like a betrayal, then, when she told me that she and Curran were now together. His wife had died the year before. Edie. I do not remember her very well, more taken as I always was by Curran himself. I recall her only as always ill, though Anna told me this was not the case. But to me her health was always fraying; I was afraid of her sometimes, her unknown precariousness. She collapsed once while we were at the beach at Murlough. I remember Curran's panic and my mother's quiet, steady action: calling an ambulance, setting Edie in the recovery position, holding both her hand and Curran's, like a

Renaissance scene. Anyway, she recovered. But a decade later she died, and between Anna and Curran everything changed. She told me that they had found that the limits of their friendship, once so easy in their clear demarcations, quickly blurred. At first, she said, we did not really know what was happening. I knew I loved him but I did not know I loved him.

I hated her then. Not, I still believe, out of jealousy for myself, but – how the mighty fall – for my father. I found myself taking his side; or rather *representing* him, standing in for his side, a side he'd long abandoned. I didn't complain, or argue with her, but for the remaining few days of her trip I held my affection in check, gave her so little that she was greedy even for a smile. I hated her and I hated myself, and I was strangely satisfied.

She returned to Belfast after a week. The night before she left she gave a poetry reading in a local bookshop. Her work was now well known, even in the US, and she drew a small crowd, both of students and visitors from nearby – one couple travelled 150 miles all the way from New York. I was there, of course, and Oki too, and despite the antagonism I was nourishing, I experienced the complicated pride and embarrassment of my mother's minor celebrity. Oki took the piss, kindly in his way, once Anna had gone home. You are a mummy's boy, he said, laughing, when we met for a drink a few days later. I didn't know what to say. Oki threw his arm around me. It's alright, he said.

I had been waiting for these moments, preparing for them. My self-containment had trained me for Oki; both in the desire I now felt flooding me, unbidden and perhaps, I was not yet sure, unwelcome, but also in my ability to turn myself inward, to transform my emotion into a flat emptiness, alchemy in reverse. I hid, as much from myself as from him. The year passed without articulation, without even a hint emerging in the open space of our interaction, though by the following summer my dreams were haunted by longing, darkened by a greed that was animal, vigorous.

For the record, I had relationships with a few women, girls really, nineteen, twenty years old, like me, as uncertain of themselves as I was. Any intimacy was always awkward, hesitant, a fumbling towards something never quite reached. Only with one girl, a sophomore from San Diego called Julia, did I find something disrupting, a longing that extended beyond a few weeks. She was dark, swarthy; her skin seemed to change colour every week as the sun dropped on it. Her green, bright eyes moved lightly, quickly. We found a freedom with each other I had never experienced before. She loved my accent, my round vowels as she used to call them, and the way, so she said, I raised my voice at the end of sentences even when they weren't questions. We laughed together a lot. She was quick to be amused, and it freed me, drew out of me a similar opening to laughter. I was almost surprised at how much I was able to enjoy myself. We were together for most of my second year.

At the end of the year Oki announced he was returning to Ghana for the summer. His grandmother was old and frail, and he wanted to see her before she died. He invited me to join him. I had agreed already to

travel to Central America with Julia. We were going
to Guatemala, to Honduras and El Salvador, working
on farms to earn our way. I declined Oki's offer, but it
grated on me, and I began to return to Oki in my dreams,
dreams that had for a long time been, if not peaceful,
at least largely empty of his presence. But it crept back,
the palpable, physical sensation of desire; increasingly at
night I would awaken, sweating, breathing tightly, and if
Julia was with me she would ask what the matter was. I
would shake my head, silently, and drink a glass of water
as though swallowing poison.

Oki left for Ghana early in June, and Julia and I for
Guatemala shortly after. It was a brutal summer. The
heat in Central America was unbearable, and we were
staying in small cabins filled with hot, stale air. We did
not so much fight, exactly, as exchange our humour
for silence; we retreated inward, each to our own dark
story. I stopped, after a while, asking about Julia's feel-
ings, aware that such a concern would open up questions
about my own, for which I could not account, even to
myself. He was everywhere; as I pulled plants from the
ground, or hacked at the crops I was harvesting, I would
find a rhythm, and into that rhythm would move Oki.
It was not simply an image, a picture that would appear
before me, of his face or his body. It was a more visceral,
tentative sensation, a spreading; Oki would move along
my nerves, push to the edge of my body, as though, as I
experienced in one nightmare, I was a host being eaten
at from within.

Julia moved from concern to anger, and began, fairly
enough, to push me for reasons for my reticence, my

withdrawal. And I had none, had nothing; nothing
that made sense. In the end I left early, before we even
reached El Salvador. I hitched from the farm we were on,
near Olanchito, all the way to San Pedro, riding in the
back of pick-ups and station wagons. I sat alone, or occasionally with peasants and farm workers, who offered me
cigarettes that I declined. I tried to tease out the various
strands of my desire. I thought that by forcing them into
words, even words that existed only in my own head,
they might become more manageable. The journey took
twenty-four hours. The *campesinos* who sat across from
me watched my flat gringo face, my concentration; the
kinder ones asked me, in halting English, if I was okay.
I nodded, lied. It did not work. There were no words
that would stick long enough to the fleeting mess of my
sensations, and I lurched from impression to impression,
each shaking off my attempt to capture it.

I flew back to New York, and took the train into the
city. I had nowhere to be, nowhere to go, and thought I
might spend a few days there before returning north. I
called a friend who lived in the Bronx; he was away for
a week, but told me where I could pick up a spare key. I
pushed open the front door of his tiny apartment, threw
my bag on the bed – the apartment was one room – and
left immediately. I wanted to be alone, but I wanted it in
company. It was late, the bars closing already. I wandered
the streets aimlessly. Music blared from garages; outside
them groups of men and women sat talking and smoking. On a sidewalk in front of a rundown tower block
I remember an old couple dancing a rhumba, watched
by four or five feral-looking children, transfixed utterly.

I walked past a tall, gaunt white man talking loudly to himself, semi-coherent. I heard the phrase repeat as I left him behind: you can have anything you don't want. I felt myself enlarge as I took it all in, my limits swell to include the mayhem of the city. Over the following days I walked it all, miles on miles. I loved the pulsing havoc, the dissonant music of the streets; but found myself drawn again and again into galleries, museums. I had gone on a field trip to the Met during the first year of college, but my experience had been curtailed by the demands of the course, my focus directed. I wanted to see what I would discover if I wandered on instinct. I lingered among the traditional African masks: the stark, bold beauty of the elongated features, their remarkable emotionality, far beyond what I had expected. I loved being able to move from these rooms to the Picassos upstairs, their unashamed theft of the forms and shapes below, their colonial homage, a complication of love and plunder. I sat in a darkened room and watched Resnais and Marker's astonishing film, *Les Statues meurent aussi*, still bold and provocative eighty years later. I walked without direction or chronology, and tried to ignore the labels on the artworks, to see what I would be drawn to without prodding, without the cheating of knowledge. I returned repeatedly to a British painting from the early 1800s by Henry Raeburn, an artist I didn't then know, of three children. One, a young boy, sits awkwardly on a pony, half turned to face the viewer. To the right of the pony, watching the boy, are another boy and a girl, both a little older. They are watching not the viewer, or the painter, but the boy on the pony, and both of their expressions display a subtle concern, as though they are worried about something that cannot be seen, or named, and is certainly not evident anywhere in the painting. The light is soft; the girl's dress, a draped white chiffon, hangs on her in loose, unfussy folds. She carries a strange rounded basket, opened at the front, but too dark to see inside. I know this painting so well now. I returned to it each time I visited that week, and was almost shocked when it struck me, on my third visit, that what I was seeing felt like my own childhood.

At the end of the summer I returned to Belfast, my first trip home since leaving for America. Anna and Curran had decided on marriage. It was just over a year from when she'd visited me. I remember calling my father, to ask him if he knew. He didn't – they weren't really in touch by then at all – and he gave away nothing when I told him. He lived alone, was still preaching in the same mission hall, though he wasn't working with the cars any more. He'd moved to a different house once his youngest moved out. He asked me if I was coming back for the wedding. I told him I wasn't sure. It was a strange conversation; I remember us saying very little but some connection, some sympathy emerging, in both directions. Conspirators in loss.

You can stay with me if you like, he said. The *if you like* felt important.

I did, though. I told Anna I'd be there but that I'd be staying with my father. I know that hurt her. I knew then too, but I couldn't help myself. She didn't say anything, didn't complain, but the gap widened, that extra pause, the tentativeness. They had, I knew, set a date for the end of the summer so that I could be there before term started. It did not incline me towards generosity.

I flew home at the end of August. I went straight to Orr's from the airport. His new place was still in east Belfast, less than a mile from where he'd lived before. He'd said it was small, but I hadn't expected it to be that small, that contained. It almost felt deliberate, that he was trying to prove something to someone, or himself. Still, it looked well – flowers and plants and pictures, clean air and tidy. A woman's touch, one suspected. He confirmed he had a young Polish cleaner who came in once a fortnight and looked after it.

I am not as young as I used to be.

I believe that's how it works, I said.

He took me out for a meal on that first evening. I don't believe we'd ever gone for a meal before. He'd turned up at birthday parties, came to watch me play football a few times; the stuttering articulations of a distant father. But sitting across from him, across a table with a lit candle, felt like an almost unspeakable intimacy. He wasn't blind then, I should say. He wasn't yet sixty, his faculties in full motion. He asked me about university, about studying, about women. I answered, loosening up on a beer, two. I found myself wanting to tell him, wanting to share, up to a point. There was a softness in him that had not previously been there, or that I, at any rate, had not noticed. I found myself longing for some kind of affirmation, for an approval, but could not be sure entirely what form that would take, or what satisfaction I would have from it.

I remember checking my phone when I got home and seeing two missed calls from Oki. As I looked up Orr was watching me.

I know what that look is, Sam, he said. Call her back.

The blunt beat of my stupid heart as he climbed the stairs.

They got married in the countryside, in a converted barn, a kind of picturesque secular church. During the meal I sat on one side of Anna, Curran on the other. I watched people watch us, bemused. Many of them had not seen me before, some hadn't even known Anna had a child. I hated myself for it, but the self-consciousness ate away at me all evening. It drew me back into myself, into my hurt, my – sure, why not? – disfiguration. I took a taxi back to Orr's before the party was done. He was still awake, sitting downstairs, reading his bible and listening to Miles Davis. For what felt like the first time all day, I smiled.

I sat down in a chair opposite and told him I didn't want to talk. You'd hardly have called Orr sensitive, but there was a generosity in his refusal to get embarrassed or uncertain; he simply sat there, reading on, and I closed my eyes. I do not often remember my dreams, but I remember that night's. Orr had set a blanket around me, and I woke in the early hours with a taste of blood, metallic, in my mouth, and the image, solitary and unattached, of an animal – a wolf perhaps, something fanged – dead at my feet.

When I returned to America I couldn't settle. My everyday life was the same; my mother's marriage did not

change anything concrete, practical. I had talked to her
rarely enough in the previous year, and she had not often
taken up time in my thoughts. But I realised, even if I
could not have articulated it at the time, that she had
always been there, a kind of invisible anchor, allowing me
a certain freedom of movement without the fear of ever
getting truly, dangerously lost. I did not care much for
Belfast, and my sense of belonging was sufficiently loose
to permit me to settle anywhere; but Anna had been my
home, and I felt – I am not naive to the whinging absurdity – that she was no longer *mine*. I was newly alone.

On a Saturday morning four weeks after I returned
from Ireland I was in bed reading. Oki barged into the
bedroom. It was October, the air cold outside, autumn
nudging towards winter. I could look from my window
at the season changing, leaves dying into bursts of colour.
I had had a number of opportunities to move into a
shared house with fellow students, but I loved the view
from my window, and the anonymity of the dorms; I
was still in the same room I had moved into when I first
arrived.

    Get up, Oki said, agitated.

    Nice to see you, Oki.

    Seriously. Stop fucking around. We have to go. Oki
was pacing from the door to the window. Those fucking
assholes, he said.

    Which ones?

    Come on, he said.

    Oki, I said. Sit down.

    Oki stared at me. Where a smile would normally

break across his face, realising his unnecessary exuberance, a scowl still hung.

I relented. Where are we going?

New York. They're deporting my brother.

I closed my book, set it down. Why?

Oki shrugged. I don't know. That's what they do.

What are we going to do? I asked him.

Oki stopped pacing, stood in the centre of the room. How the fuck do I know? Are you coming?

I nodded.

There's a train in half an hour. I'll meet you downstairs in five minutes. He grabbed a towel and threw it at me.

Oki's brother lived in Harlem, a few blocks from the train station. The train was delayed on the way there, and it was early afternoon by the time we arrived. His apartment was small, cramped; paint cracked on the walls. The smell of Indian food floated through from the apartment next door; the windows seemed porous, the cold air streaming in. Oki and I sat on the two chairs in the kitchen. The table was sticky. Jonathan, Oki's brother, stood beside his girlfriend, a Dominican woman a couple of years older than him, who introduced herself as Jasmin. She stared at Oki with what seemed utter disdain.

Jonathan listed off complaints as though memorising for a test. They deprivated me a proper lawyer, he said. They deprivated me a chance to make my case. They deprivated me for no reason.

I watched Oki bite his tongue. What did they get you for? He was careful to use his brother's language.

Nothing. Made up.

What though? Oki asked. He was younger than Jonathan, by five years. He was used to this, I could see; of wearing his achievements lightly so as not to upset the traditional balance, of choosing his questions cautiously. On the few occasions Oki had mentioned his brother, the picture he had painted had been quite different. I was conscious of being brought into something, into a new relation, a confidence.

Jonathan walked to the window, ignored Jasmin's arm reaching out to him as he passed her. Drugs, he said.

Trucks rumbled along outside, rattling the windows as though contributing to the conversation.

But they made it up? Oki said.

Jonathan looked out the window, peering up and down the street, staring purposefully. He didn't answer.

It was hardly any, Jasmin said.

I could see Oki's anger. So now what? Oki asked.

Now he has to leave the country in three weeks, she said. Unless you can do something.

Oki threw back her disgust. Unless I can do something? He fairly spat the *I*.

I excused myself, requested the bathroom. I stood inside, listening through the thin door as the accusations began to grow, Oki being blamed for everything, his success a form of betrayal, as Jasmin had it. I emerged to see Oki stand up, shaking his head.

I came because I thought you'd been treated unfairly. But you haven't. There's nothing I can do.

Jonathan turned from the window and looked at his brother. Fuck you, he said.

Oki picked up his bag, nodded to me.

We walked down the stairs, out into the street. Jonathan leaned out of the window. Fuck you, Oki. I don't need you. His voice carried. People turned around, followed the sound. Oki stopped for a moment, looked up, then walked on. Fuck you, the voice at his back continued. You piece of shit. You fucking piece of shit.

We hardly spoke on the train home. Oki simmered, his anger close to the surface for a couple of hours, but by the time we reached Troy it had dissipated, and a melancholy had taken over. Let's get a drink, I said.

We went to a small bar on the fringe of the campus. We chased beers with shots, round after round, and by midnight both of us were well drunk. Oki lurched from moments of introspection, his head lowered, barely moving, to flights of bold declaration, anger beating a path through his thick verbs, mocking and hurt. I moved around the edges of his conversation, more padding than responding. I watched him and saw, for what seemed to me the first time, how raw and present were his wounds. Oki had always held himself with such swagger, such apparent freedom, that it was startling to realise how much he too was carrying. His family, I learned, had not paved the way for him to come to the US to study, as he had previously implied, but had rather felt it as unfaithfulness, and had paid him little attention since. They blamed him too, now, for his brother's increasing difficulties; Jonathan, though older, had followed Oki a year after his arrival, but had abandoned his studies after just a few months, and lived thereafter on shaky ground, his student visa now legally useless. He had moved to New York and barely saw Oki, drifting in and out of informal jobs, soon disappearing almost entirely from his brother's life, popping up – often unannounced – when he needed money or, once, when he was on the run from a dealer in DC, where he had been staying for a few months. Oki helped him out where he could, but still his family blamed him for Jonathan's transformation, his increasing isolation.

We staggered home, Oki much the worse for wear, leaning heavily on me. Oki was six foot two, almost half a foot taller, and we must have made a strange pair stumbling along College Square, a four-legged lopsided beast. Oki pulled up, asked me where I was taking him.

Home, I said.

My house is too far, he said. I'll stay at yours tonight.

I hesitated, briefly but consciously, and wondered later whether if I had given myself a little longer might I have worked it out; might the strength required, or the weakness, whatever, have come to me.

We cut across the square, to my dorm block. I switched on the light. Oki switched it off again immediately.

Jesus, Sam, he said. It's the middle of the fucking night. He laughed as he said it.

He pulled off his shirt and trousers and dropped on to the bed. I watched him, watched his scar hidden in the virtual darkness, felt I could see it even though I could barely see anything. I took my shirt off, and pulled out a sleeping bag from the wardrobe. I threw it on the ground and lay down on top of it.

He sat up. What are you doing? he said. I'm not going to kick you out of your bed. You can sleep here too.

It's alright, I said.

He spoke louder. Fuck, Sam, I'll sleep on the floor then. You're not sleeping in a sleeping bag in your own room.

I'll put it away, I said.

Oki lay back down, turned his body to the wall. I lay down on the other side of the bed, hearing myself breathing, feeling that it was giving me away. We lay there in silence, me on my back, Oki facing the wall. I stared at the ceiling, the blackness slowly giving way to shifting greys and blues, my eyes adjusting, calibrating. I remembered, as a child, being on a bus with my mother, somewhere in France, in the country, late at night. I was staring out the window when the driver turned off the internal lights, and the sky, which just a second before had been a black smear, flooded suddenly with light, stars flung messily to every corner.

I turned my head towards him, and saw the scar, the light skin upon the dark, a line flat now before me. I could not take my eyes away, and a feeling of sympathy hit me, not for Oki nor even for myself, but for all the people I had hated for refusing the temptation of my own. I reached out my hand and ran my fingers along it, a ridge where the skin had healed. I held my breath as I did so, waited for his reaction, his anger. But it did not come, and he curved, I was sure, his body ever so slightly towards me. I flattened my hand out, took up more of his back. I heard him breathing now, the slight quickening, the air coming in stronger, faster. I pressed heavier, unmistakable, and still he didn't react, or reacted by not reacting, and my own breathing almost stopped, slowed to a still, long moment. I leaned over and put my mouth to the line, moved my lips along it. I moved my hand down his back, found the small valley at the top of his ass. I moved further still, under his boxers, the elastic giving as my hand went further, between and within. He tightened but stayed where he was, his breathing now slowing, sinking. I moved myself closer, finding him with my body, the gap closed. I moved my hand around and found his cock, already growing, and edged it through the gap in his boxers. I played the length of it with my fingers, gentle, and felt the weight rise in my hand. I moved my lips now to his neck, his ear, and still he said nothing, still did not turn, but let it happen. I pulled on him, my hand full and tight, and felt him push back, moving to my movement, joining me, participating. His chest moved, the air filling his lungs faster and stronger. He breathed louder, and I pressed myself into his neck as we moved quicker. He came in less than a minute, the low groan escaping him as though forced out, like an animal dying. He did not move though, did not speak, did not turn to me. I stayed where I was for half a minute more, pressed closely to him, still holding his cock as it retreated. I waited for something from him, anything, but he remained closed off, silent. I moved back, let go, and lay where I was before. I put my hand, wet now, on my own stomach, and stared again at the ceiling. The excitement gave way to an emptiness, flat, and I lay there unmoving until, ten minutes later, I was sure that he was asleep.

I got up and walked the corridor to the bathroom. I washed my hands, my face. The mirror threw back more fear than I had imagined. I stared at myself for a minute, two minutes, but could not put words together in a way to make a coherent thought, except to realise that not putting words together made thinking difficult, an irony that at another time might have amused me. I did not know what to do next, whether to return to the room or not. I waited five minutes and then retraced my steps along the corridor, committing myself to the truth of what had just taken place. I pushed open the door, and though it took a few moments for my eyes to adjust again to the darkness, I knew immediately that Oki was gone.

The next morning I woke late. There was a lawnmower going already below my window; I remembered that I was supposed to be working. I quickly threw on clothes, splashed water on my face, and ran to the outhouse.

The rota had me in the main college square, but because I was late someone else had been sent there. I was grateful to be exiled to the back fields. By the time I returned, later than my hours demanded, everyone else had packed up. The shed was locked, and I realised I had left my key at home. I didn't want to leave the tools unattended, so I drove the mower across the campus to the dorms, half a mile away. As I passed the science buildings I saw Oki emerge, with a girl I didn't recognise. He looked up and spotted me – I was no more than thirty yards away, and driving towards him – and I waved. He didn't respond. Instead he said something to her, handed her his bag, and moved quickly back inside the building.

I kept driving, and drew level with her. I nodded as I
passed, and she smiled back, nonchalant, careless. When
I reached the end of the street, another fifty yards further
along, I turned to see Oki and the girl walking in the
other direction. He had his arm around her.

I spent the evening preparing for a test on the Monday,
and waiting for some contact. My mobile sat in front
of me, taunting in its silence. I moved back and forth
in my own mind, from decision to decision, but could
not, when it came to it, hit the button. I slept roughly,
jarring awake three or four times, alert and expectant.
There was no fear; it was a steady, austere certainty, hope
draining slowly, blood through a pinprick.

   I didn't see Oki all week. I thought, obviously, of nothing else. I began to wonder what had actually happened,
the repetition in my mind breaking down, moving
between memory and imagination, until I was uncertain
which of the pictures I returned to were true. Oki's skin,
though, the smooth dark surface of him, was irrefutable.

   On the following Saturday I walked to his apartment.
It was early, a little after eight. For the first time the
ground had a thin grey-white crust; it crunched as I
walked. I had a key, but didn't use it. I knocked, at first
lightly, then with more force. After a couple of minutes
Oki opened. He looked startled, as though he had not
expected to see me ever again.

   What? he said. The door was only slightly ajar. He
did not open it further. Most of his body remained out
of sight.

   Are we going to talk?

He shook his head. About what?

Oki, I said.

There's nothing to talk about. He looked behind him.

I could feel my heart pounding in my chest. I'd always imagined that was a cliché.

Look, Sam ... Oki paused, stuck for words. Nothing happened.

It did, I said.

Oki moved forward, his hand reaching towards me. Even as I write this I watch it come, and feel a shock of joy before it touches me. I stumble back a few yards. Oki moving out now, into the corridor. He is wearing only underwear. It fucking didn't, he says, maybe. I'm not sure. Oki's fist hits me in the face as the words come out, and I fall, crumple almost. Another cliché: slow motion. Everything slackening. Oki's foot in my diaphragm, pain the only speed, everything else heavy, sluggish.

It didn't last long, I suppose. I walk home, my ribs – one broken, I later find out – press against something inside, and I fear a rupture. The sky is dull, like lead, and I remember other skies, other days, like this one but not like this one. I am strangely satisfied. I had it coming, I think to myself. I had it coming. I taste blood in my mouth – literally for once – and swallow it. I raise my hand to my face, and remember, for the first time in months, and I am back in my mother's bedroom, and the pain gets taken up, lifted into another pain. One pain becomes another. *Plus ça change.*

•

Philip was dead. Inasmuch as absence is death. In the weeks after the attack (a spade's a spade) he was hunted, the law and social media in unholy alliance. But to no effect. He was sixteen, and it was thought to be inevitable, a matter of time, that he would appear, either of his own volition or by the simple mistake of allowing himself to be seen. But he wasn't. No CCTV revealed him, no cash machines, no passports. He vanished, sucked up into the air like Christ himself. What these days and weeks were like I know only second-hand, of course – even by the time I was old enough to understand, the stories had collected themselves into a sort of opaque myth, and the surfaces I scratched at revealed more about Orr and Anna's respective ways of dealing than they did Philip himself.

Anna encouraged me to talk about it, to speak of what I remembered, what I feared, what I hated. Perhaps she saw it growing in me, the event accreting, layer upon layer. I was so young that it didn't happen only once but rather kept happening, each moment of recollection, as my vocabulary grew, not simply a retelling but a re-enactment, the words themselves palpable, structural. The randomness – *something happened to me* – gave way, over and over again, to sharper, more brutal redescriptions, more specificity. For Anna, at least if I could speak it the less would those words own me, burn themselves through me.

Not so Orr. I saw him less, of course, growing up. Sometimes, for months, not at all. Still, when I did, confusion carried; the bluntness with which he spoke to Anna was avoided with me. I do not know, even now,

how much of that was a result of Philip's actions. I was too
young, of course, to remember how he treated me when
I was an infant, though I have a vague, hazy sense of genuine affection. There is something that exists for me, too
insubstantial to be called a memory, of his face and mine
in correspondence, my smile learned from his, an unarticulated kindness; even – God help me – devotion. But
after the event (event?), I remember (remember?) only
reticence, a hushed stillness on his part. I do not know
how much of this is my perception – when I looked at
Orr did I see Philip? – or perhaps instead, or as well, he
could not see me without seeing Philip, and what must
that have done to him, what necessities of restraint must
that have involved him in? Philip, in his absence, became
more present than he could have imagined. Or a further
perhaps – I raise my hat – he knew this perfectly. Philip
the mediator. *Except a grain of wheat fall into the ground and
die, it abides alone; but if it die, it bears much fruit.*

But the boy himself, the body, the person – he was
gone. I asked Orr once, much later – just before, in fact,
he came to live with me in Brooklyn – if he had looked
for Philip. I mean, beyond the conversations with the
police and so on. He stared blankly out of the window
in the room we were sitting in, high up on the side of
the Cavehill, with views – not that he could see them –
down on to Belfast Lough, and told me that, for the year
and a half after he disappeared, he would walk out once
or twice a week, the same time of the day, in the belief
that Philip was watching. He would stalk the same route,
setting himself up, making of himself a target. He was
convinced, he said, that he would appear, emerge from

some alley with a poised violence, a wail of anger. He knew, he said, that Philip's ambition was him, Orr, and not me, that the *wrath* – I remember this word – he had enacted already would not be sufficient to him.

But there was no appearance, no showing up. Nothing. The police, after the requisite few weeks, had opened a missing-persons case, but after a year of no sightings, they shelved it. Not closed it entirely; but it was widely suspected that whatever anger Philip had directed towards me had been converted into guilt, and that he had enacted on himself the remainder of the violence he had within him. Anna accepted this wisdom, or perhaps affected to accept it, providing as it did a line underneath it of sorts, even if only in pencil. Orr, however, did not. He resisted the shrug, the giving up, and though there was little else he could do, he still carried some expectation of return.

I grew up, then, surrounded by nothing, but feeling the weight of it. Philip I remembered as a fairy-tale figure, the beckoning finger in the tale that promised and threatened at the same time, painted the picture and scored it out. I do not wish to make too much of this – *I know* – but it is hard to draw the lines, the connections between things, when the things themselves have such little form. The one thing I knew was that Philip was gone. My face was his last act, and then he disappeared, and was never seen again. At least, I knew that until Orr – as I was about to leave that afternoon – took my arm and pulled me back down on to the bench beside him and told me to wait. There was more.

*

It was never easy with Orr. So many expectations in the first few years of his moving here were overturned that it felt at times like violence; as though, in my pre-conceptions being proved wrong, my father was actively correcting me. It was not like this, of course. I had, nat-urally perhaps, but unfairly, built a version of my father that was crueller, less interesting, than he turned out to be. But it had still pained, this encroachment of the real Orr into the image I had, and had been content with.

He moved here, I should explain, because he was alone. His sight had begun to blur in his early sixties. He had ignored it at first, and continued to live as he had before, still preaching, pastoring, carrying himself with his regular swagger. But week by week things became more difficult, and eventually a young woman at the church, a nurse, spotted him struggling to read. He had got by for so long pretending because he knew the texts so well he could quote them. Within six months he had lost all the vision in his left eye, and 50 per cent in his right. He took it with good humour – *we see through a glass, darkly* – but he knew the direction it was all head-ing, and knew the comedy would be more difficult to sustain. I had not been to Belfast in a few years but I made a trip home, a couple of months after I found out. I asked him – his vision almost gone entirely by this point, already making his way around with a stick – if he blamed God. Your God, I asked, if he blamed your God. You're fond of that possessive pronoun, aren't you? he said, and when I ignored the jibe, he continued, blunt as you like: He's taken everything else. Why not my eyes?

He still had, by the doctor's final assessment, around

7 per cent vision in his right eye. It was a number that pleased him: a holy number. His sermons had been fairly flooded with sevens – the seven fat years and seven lean, the seven days of creation (the rest day is counted, he was always pleased to point out to the workaholics), the seven devils who left Mary Magdalene. Every seventh year was a sabbath – forgive debts, he counselled, and took his own counsel – and after seven sevens came fifty, the jubilee, when the land itself was set free, returned. How many times shall I forgive my brother? Seven times? No: multiply.

And so he saw shapes still, blurred movement, hazy and dark, like old film footage layered on itself, he described it, one body becoming another. It was not enough, though – he could neither cross roads safely nor shop for food without someone to help, and even his own home became a trap, stairs and seats and doorways unidentifiable. His youngest had already emigrated to Australia, and Anna was with Curran, not that that was ever a realistic avenue, I suppose. So he moved in with his remaining son, who lived in a sizeable house just outside Belfast. It was a compromised scenario though, Orr's loss of independence more difficult for him than he had expected. He was given a room at the rear of the house, next to their two children, both teenagers, and whilst they liked him, and he them, their mother had never had much time for her father-in-law, and was not slow to let him know. She bickered with her children for spending too much time with him instead of studying, and he spent more and more time in his room on his own, listening to radio shows and audiobooks. The older

boy tried to teach him braille: I'll not live long enough
to get the benefit, he said. When the family finally proposed a nursing home – Orr had been living with them
for almost two years – the collective relief could have
lifted the *Hindenburg*.

He moved into a fold off the Antrim Road. He was
nudging towards his late sixties and, his eyes aside, he
was healthy and sharp. He could not get used to it. The
rest of the residents – inmates, he called them, when
he spoke to me by phone, which was more and more
frequently – were older, frail and tired, mostly humour-
less. Half of them didn't know who they were. He had,
at first, looked forward to the company, but it proved a
false hope, and he spent even more time alone, his world
closing in on him, getting smaller and smaller. He felt
himself reduce; for the first time in his life, it was all too
much. He was in the wrong place.

   He had been in the home for six months by the time I
visited again. Another few years had passed and still I did
not look forward to returning. It always felt to me like a
retreat; it would take me weeks afterwards to shake the
Belfast shit off myself, to climb back into the thin, clean
air of my American life. My mother had been again for
a visit, a few months before, this time accompanied by
Curran. I had thought about her often, more than I let
myself realise. I held it against her. I was embarrassed, I
suppose – or perhaps embarrassed is not quite right. She
who had always been there, she who knew everything – I
could not forgive her that.

   At that stage I was in Gowanus, a pretty shitty one-bed

walk-up, the price of my privacy. They stayed in a hotel in midtown, but came across to pick me up one evening, and my mother looked around my apartment as though it were an exhibition in itself. Her ignorance and interest combined to give me something back, a sense of myself as unknown, and I loved her for it. In my childhood her questions had felt like prompts, the narrative predetermined; if there were answers she already had them, and I might hope at best to stumble into some approximation. But I realised, as she scanned my bookshelves, stared with puzzlement at cheap paintings and sculptures I'd bought at degree shows or from friends, that I had begun to find my own corners, my own periphery. My outer reaches. Darkness as character – the unknown not an absence but a space to grow into.

I watched Curran look at paintings, and could not help but share his joy, his thrilled uncool exuberance. I had been working at the Met for a few years by this stage; still only a guard, but already getting noticed, my own attention to detail and evident love of the art catching the wonderful American meritocratic eye. Curran's childish pleasure turned out to be an inadvertent generosity; I remember noticing, after they left, a confidence in my choices, my namings, that could only have come from him.

When I returned to Belfast, then, I could have stayed with my mother, but out of a mixture of curiosity and independence, I suppose, I booked myself into a cheap hotel in the city centre for the five days I was planning to stay. I arrived late on the first night, and walked alone

to the Cathedral Quarter. I had kept in touch with no
one from home save my parents, so I had no one to call.
I could have trawled through Facebook, but in truth,
and as usual, the anonymity appealed. I had a drink in a
bar I had visited once or twice with my mother when I
was still a teenager, her buying me rum-and-Cokes and
laughing at my hesitation, my fear of getting caught. I
sat on my own, listened to the conversations floating
unattached around me, the dropped phrases and thick
vowels reminding me of who I was, who I tried not to
be. At one stage a woman shuffled up to the bar, money
for her round already in her hand. She wore a low-cut
dress, breasts barely being held back from their threatened freedom. I tried not to look.

Alright love, she said. Early thirties, a bit older than
me. I nodded, smiled. Not bad, eh?

I must have raised my eyebrows, because she pushed
her chest out a little more, and laughed.

You're new here, she said. I can tell.

Can you?

That accent. You pick that up halfway across the
Atlantic?

Something like that.

Are you American?

No such luck. I felt myself squeeze back into the
words, the metre.

A turncoat, eh? Did you live over there?

Still do. New York.

Fuck me. New York. I fucking love New York. She
raised her hand to her mouth, eyebrows jumping. Sorry.
Are you good living?

Good enough. But not like that.

Thank Christ, she said, pleased with her own joke.

I laughed. I began to relax, felt something happen that I rarely experienced in America. I was being flirted with, which wasn't new, not exactly, but it was with a woman, which was. They seemed to pick up on it faster there. I was letting go, enjoying the freedom, the disassociation from myself, or part of myself.

You drinking on your own? she asked me.

It's quicker, I said, and she laughed.

What are you back for?

Reality encroaching again, the ignorant beast. Oh you know. Obligation. Duty.

How long will your duties take?

Ah, it depends. I felt the air sink, flatten. In it flooded: the world, tomorrow, all of it.

She placed her order, added a pint for me. She introduced herself. We shook hands, and I considered telling her, coming clean. But what harm was there? That dogged drive to honesty, to needless explanation, how well had it served me? I thought of my father again and, not for the first time, envied him that, his unapologetic being, his selfishness. What I wouldn't give. I smiled, told her my name, said it was a pleasure meeting her and, at her prompting, promised to join her and her friends in a while.

I didn't, of course. I finished my drink and stepped out into the late-summer evening, the air still warm, night not yet fallen. I wandered over the Queen's Bridge, heading towards the new run of bars down at Titanic

Quarter. The city had spread, slowly but steadily, out
across the Lagan and into the working-class estates to
the east, driving house prices up and families out. It used
to be all flags out this way, one or the other; now cranes
hung above terraces marked for demolition, and new
half-finished apartment blocks caught the eye with their
slick surfaces and aura of money. It was hard to lament
the old, but the new felt overdone, a banker's Ferrari, an
inner turmoil not so easily displaced.

There were fewer people on the streets here than
in the centre, but the bars were still busy. I had one
more drink – this time undisturbed – and walked back
to my hotel in an unexpected fug of satisfaction, the
alcohol thinning my blood just enough, my movements
that bit looser, lighter. This place wasn't as bad as I
remembered.

I slept easily, and woke refreshed. I ate breakfast –
more flirting, this time with the young Polish woman
who served me coffee; what was it about being in Belfast
that made this so easy? – and then caught the bus at the
side of the City Hall, heading north. The nursing home
was on the Antrim Road, on a sprawling piece of garden
nestled into the lower parts of the Cavehill near Ben
Madigan. It was one of Belfast's old wealthy areas, large
houses neighbouring one another with a stolid pride,
architectural confidence. It was a safe affluence, all the
same; I didn't envy it. I wouldn't have given up my shitty
Bushwick apartment for two of them.

My father was waiting for me in his room. A carer led
me down the hallway, making small-talk. I remember
the sudden hesitation clawing at me, as though I had

only just realised why I was there. I stopped – the young man leading me stopped too, turning inquisitively – and caught my breath.

First visit? he said. I nodded. Take your time, he said. He pointed down the corridor. Room 23, when you're ready. He patted me on the shoulder as he walked away.

I turned and looked out the window. Belfast Lough lay a mile below, the northern suburbs sprawling easy between, green and lush at the end of summer. A light rain had just started to fall but the sun was still out, and the air flickered, shone. The ferry to Scotland inched along in front of Holywood, and I watched it, and was returned to the few summers my mother had taken me to the Highlands on that very boat, Pitlochry and Aviemore and Fort William. I recalled her telling me – I had been eating ice cream at the time, ten years old – that I may have been conceived there, in a cabin near Elgin, and remembered my horror at the thought that I had been conceived at all, whatever that was.

I moved down the corridor. I knocked on my father's door and waited for a voice. Come in, I heard, and pushed it open. My father sat on his bed, his hands resting on either side of him, as though holding him up. He was dressed well enough, and his hair was combed, flattened, but he was haggard, his cheeks falling in on themselves. I could hardly believe it. He looked at me.

Who is it? he said. Nico, is that you? Is my son here yet?

I'm your son, I said.

A smile crept on to his face, recognition.

There he is, he said. Nice to see you. He laughed, and

his face changed, the gaunt hollow replaced with the charm, the cheek that I remembered. Well, come on in then. Welcome to my kingdom.

I looked around the room, took it in, the flowered curtains, the banal browns and creams. I was faintly relieved my father couldn't see, God knows what he'd have thought of it if he could. Still, he must have known where he was. He'd visited enough of these places before he went blind.

As though I had spoken aloud, Orr said, Probably better that I can't see it. He still held a smile, and I was surprised at finding myself grateful to him for making this less sombre than it might have been.

You always loved beige, right? I said.

He tried to push himself up but didn't have it in his arms. What about a cuppa? he said.

We sat opposite one another in the common room, at a table beside the window. The view stretched from the lough below around to the northern side, where the zoo used to be. In the distance I could see the war memorial at Knockagh.

Nice view? Orr said.

Yeah.

Describe it for me.

Sure you remember it, don't you? I was conscious of being looked at but not seen. I remembered the feeling from the last time I was back, but I had hidden it away in the meantime, and I was surprised that such an unnerving sensation could be so easily displaced in memory.

Words are my eyes now, he said.

So we talked. Slowly, gently, one small offering and then another, an exchange first of descriptions, then of kindnesses, then of hurts. This is when he told me about Philip, his desire to lure him out. A routine, an expectation. He spoke also about Anna, a frank ruefulness he had never before expressed. They took shape that day, for me; their solitariness, as I had mostly known it, temporarily overturned by stories, articulated affections, until a picture became present, actual; as Orr spoke I found something release in me, a sort of unanticipated acquittal of myself, enlarged by the capacity they had between them, even if only briefly, created in the world.

We talked for hours. He was wise enough not to pry too much into the detail of my life, though I had not expected him to remember as much as he did. I found myself stunned by my enjoyment, bitter almost that it should feel so easy.

As I went to leave he pulled me back down on to the bench.

I have not told you everything, he said. I have not told even Anna. Philip is not dead. At least, he was not dead, he was not dead then. You were still a boy, he said, nine or ten, when he came back. He'd have been twenty-one. I had given up by then, of course. I was preaching, a wee hall in Larne. The service was halfway through, the singing just finished, and I got up behind the pulpit. Raised up a little – you could see everyone. And I started reading from the text – Paul's letter to the Ephesians: And you hath he quickened, who were dead in trespasses and sins; Wherein in time past ye walked according to the course of this world, according to the

prince of the power of the air, the spirit that now work-
eth in the children of disobedience . . . And I looked up
at that point, and I remember the pure shock of it, to
see him sitting in the back row, staring at me. His face
was stone, flawless. I know this will sound ridiculous,
but I thought immediately of how *beautiful* he was. And
I did not know what to do. I went on reading, finished
the text. I could barely get through it in places: But now
in Christ Jesus ye who sometimes were far off are made
nigh by the blood of Christ. I was being mocked. When I
had finished reading I prayed, as I do, and when I opened
my eyes he was gone. I stared at his empty seat and I
could not believe it. And then the sound from outside: a
crash, glass shattering. I jumped down into the aisle and
ran to the back door. My car was parked right outside
the church, on the pavement; a rock through the front
windscreen. I couldn't see him. I walked around the car,
into the street, looking for him. A few of the elders had
come outside and asked if I was okay. Then they saw
the car. I could not believe I had not come down from
the pulpit as soon as I saw him. Embraced him. I started
shouting his name. I can't remember what else I shouted.
The poor people from the hall had no idea, they didn't
know what to do. One started to call the police and I
made him put his phone away. I shouted and shouted for
Philip to come out, to talk to me. But he didn't. He was
gone again.

He stopped speaking and sat still, silent. I sat beside
him, empty of responses. Eventually he spoke again.

That was it. The only time I saw him again. I believe
he came to do me violence but couldn't see it through.

Something in him resisted. He did not have the measure
of it.

I looked across the room at him now, a Bushwick timber
yard buzzing in the background, and remembered that
conversation, remembered my decision to invite him
to New York to live with me. I went to see Anna that
night, had dinner with her and Curran. I had made
no commitment of secrecy to Orr, but in the end I
did not tell her what we had spoken about. I thought
about it, alone in my hotel room, the young drunks of
Belfast loudly crowding the streets below as I stared
down. Invented scenarios bled one into another, and
eventually I gave up imagining what would happen and
gave myself over to the desire, the unexpected enthu-
siasm. I proposed the idea when I returned to see him
on the following morning. I allowed him a couple of
days to consider it, but he told me later he had decided
immediately. I stayed on for an extra week, making
the necessary enquiries, applications. He had a friend
who worked in the US Embassy in Dublin, and made
the appropriate winks and handshakes to speed up the
process. And two months later I took the subway out
to JFK and met him off the flight. So you came, I said,
and took his bags from the young airline representative
who had assisted him from the plane.

I am come that they might have life, he grinned, and
that they might have it more abundantly.

•

From the subway exit to the museum was a quarter of a mile. Six hundred and forty-two steps. I tried to force myself into a calmness, each footstep a statement. He was everywhere, I knew, but I didn't see him. I smiled to myself as I walked through the staff entrance, climbed the stairs. Balthasar approached me before I left the common room for the galleries.

How are you feeling?

I nodded. Ship-shape.

You must take care of yourself, Sam. As my grand-father used to say, there's few of us left.

The morning passed more or less without incident, though one woman in an adjoining gallery had an asthma attack and had to be assisted by a medic, which caused a small scene. It heightened the experience for the other viewers, I again observed; they could never be sure that the unfortunate woman had not been made unwell simply by the art, and it charged their own experience with a potential danger. I had wondered, at times, if we shouldn't perhaps set up this kind of thing every now and again, an unofficial service to our visitors. Rembrandt while healthy is one thing; but with the subtle threat of illness, even death, in the air, what it becomes. We laughed over lunch as I raised the suggestion. When I returned to the floor for the afternoon, it was with an ease, a lightness; the previous day all but erased.

It was almost five o'clock when it happened. I turned from the Van Dyck towards the Vermeer, and there he was, standing in the centre of the room, staring at me. I stopped moving, and Philip took it up, reaching out his hand as he crossed the twenty feet between us. A couple of visitors turned to see, then turned away. I let him take my hand, felt it drop again to my side. I heard words but could not attach them to things. How are you doing, long time, God, I heard you were here (you heard I was here?), well, you look well, isn't it, Vermeer's light, I know. They moved around me, but I concentrated, focused only on slowing my heart down, refinding the thump thump thump that would settle me. Philip's face, older but so clearly himself, just added to, an accretion. His scar still fairly shone; he had done a lot less than me to hide it.

We should have a coffee, Philip is saying. I hear now. A coffee, Sam, eh?

I am shaking my head.

A coffee, Sam. Jesus. Thirty-five years. Thirty-five, Sam.

I have to go, I said, eventually. I have to go.

Of course, of course, Philip said, still smiling. It's great to see you. Sure I'll come back tomorrow. We can have coffee when you finish. Like, five? Five-thirty?

I moved off quickly. I felt his eyes on my back, his stare following me. I shivered, and wondered if he spotted it, the movement. The revulsion. On an impulse I walked on, past the exit door, out through another gallery, giving away, I felt, as little information as I could about where I was going. I was pleased with myself, at my calculation; surprised at my presence of mind. I found another of the staff exits in the north wing and looked around. He had not followed. I pushed through the doorway and took the stairs, already finding the measure of myself. It had happened and yet I was still there. Nothing had ended. As I walked I began to experience almost a joy, a thrill of accomplishment, as though I had willed and implemented a plan successfully. I looked at my watch and realised I had left the galleries five minutes early. I gambled I could get away with it, and stepped into a storeroom in case anyone passed. I waited: two minutes, three, in the musty stillness of the darkened space. A few statues sat awkwardly at varying heights, swaddled tightly in bubble wrap and cardboard. I thought of my family, what passed for my family: Anna, Orr, the boys. I remembered one of the early trips we took together, to an old country house somewhere. We had walked through rooms not dissimilar to this one, and I had pointed to the strange, austere busts that policed the long halls and likened them, laughing, to my brothers.

I walked back out into the corridor a few minutes later and made my way to the common room. The mood at the end of the day was as it always was, a kind of subdued gratefulness, another day down. I scanned the faces for signs but everything was normal. Balthasar approached, but only grabbed me on the shoulder and said, Who'd have thought you could still slum it so well?

On the way to the Met the next day I walked slowly through Central Park. Even New York was sleepy on a Sunday morning, subdued and lethargic. People moved more slowly, and there were fewer of them. I walked with purpose, or so I told myself. Fear abandoned. I had one more day on the floor. I had considered making Balthasar come up with another plan, getting someone else to work the shift – it wasn't like it was my job. But I couldn't just go and hide in the office. I am no longer a child, my inner voice pleaded, and I will not be afraid of Philip Orr, nor of anyone. He has left his mark – the phrase has always been alive to me – but the past is the past. God, my unconvincing monologue; like one of those yoga exponents continually telling others, repeatedly and manically, how meditation is the answer to everything as their own lives continue to unravel, like everyone else's, around them.

The Rubenses bloomed. The flesh practically fell off them. I had been right: threat, danger enlivened the experience of the paintings, made them visceral in a way the austere silence disguised. Maybe, in a week or two, I thought, I really will approach the management, propose it. Take the paintings into the city instead of getting the city to come in. Cézanne on the subway, Holbein in a pizza joint. Van Dongen in a strip show. I was pleased – proud, even – that I had not lost my love for such a useless art form. Painting died before you were born, one of the newer, younger assistants at the Met had said to me in the beginning, I having uncharacteristically let slip my fascination. Have you been in the Rembrandt room recently? I asked him.

Still, I wondered, sometimes. Was I just holding on to the tiny sliver of the past I still had – my mother, weekends in the Antrim hills at seven, eight years old? How many of the opinions I held were my own? Did I love the early Matisse, like I said, or did I love that Curran loved the early Matisse, and had made Anna love the early Matisse, and so me too, inevitably, begat begat begat, myself?

I moved tentatively the entire day, from gallery to gallery, expecting Philip at every turn. But Philip did not appear. When the end of the day arrived I walked through the top-floor galleries, detouring through to the Impressionists, finding Marcela, as always, in front of Cézanne. We acknowledged each other without speaking, standing in front of *Mont Sainte-Victoire*. In silence the painting did its work, colour becoming form becoming satisfaction. She slipped her arm into mine.

We moved off, into the adjoining gallery, towards the stairs. Suddenly, raised voices. We turned and there he was, Philip, arguing with another guard.

There, Philip said, pointing to me.

I pulled my arm from Marcela's.

What is it? she said. Who's that?

I shook my head. Give me a minute.

I'll wait for you downstairs, she said, as I walked across the gallery.

It's alright, Hector, I said. Hector shook his head, clearly pissed off. He followed Marcela to the stairs, muttering to himself.

Sam, Philip said. I got here late, sorry. They were trying to kick me out.

The museum is closed, I said. It's their job.

I know, I know, he nodded. Anyway. Let's get a drink.

I heard the door close behind Hector. We were alone. At the far end of the galleries a woman was tidying the gift area. Two hundred and fifty feet, I guessed.

I can't, I said.

I thought we'd made a plan, Philip said, his voice catching, reining something in.

The paintings stared at us; the air thick.

Tomorrow, then, he said.

Tomorrow I'm off.

Perfect.

No.

He shook his head. No? he said. He looked around, at the paintings, the heavy red walls.

I have to go, I said. The museum is closed.

He stared at me. I felt it again, and tried to refuse it. Fear. Jesus, shame.

You have nothing to fear from me, he said, but I was already walking away. Sam, he called.

I turned, held myself, blood hurtling towards the edges of me. No, I said. No.

Alright, he said.

I watched him walk slowly away. At the entrance to the gallery he turned. I'll see you again, he said, his raised finger addressing me.

I stood on my own for a few minutes longer, listened to his footsteps descend the marble stairs. The water pitcher shimmered.

In the staff room Marcela was waiting for me. What was that?

It doesn't matter.

You have love problems?

I smiled. Not the way you're thinking. I threw on my jacket.

You look troubled, she said.

Involuntarily, I lifted my hand to my face, my scar. I noticed Marcela noticing. I had always loved that she seemed one of the few people who'd got past it quickly, who seemed able to see me and not it. I was not unaware, even as I did it, that I was forcing her to look.

I'm alright, I said, picking up my bag. But thank you.

We strode out together, into the brisk late-summer breeze. A chill was already in the air, a foretaste. We bought slices of pizza on the corner of 78th and Madison, and ate as we walked south. I felt myself relax. We turned left at the Breuer, and walked past a crowd of elderly Japanese tourists chattering excitedly in front of the Ashton. As we weaved our way through them one old woman took a step backward, almost tumbling into me. I caught her, smiling, and a ripple of laughter spread through the group, a few cheers. The woman apologised, bowing her head to me in acknowledgement. I bowed back, smiling too, and as I lifted my head, about to move on, I noticed, fifty yards behind, Philip. He was following us.

I took Marcela by the arm and pulled her towards me. What are you doing?

Trust me, please, I said. We moved swiftly across the road, just before a slew of cars rushed by after us, and she turned with me to see Philip stuck on the other side of the street, waiting for a gap. We quickly rounded the corner on to Park and I dragged us into a run, thirty feet, before ducking into a bar. I moved to the darkened front window, found a spot from which I could look out. Marcela stared at me. I motioned for her to sit down. The barman glared at us.

I raised a finger in the air: one minute. I pressed myself
against the wall, watched the street. Ten seconds passed,
twenty. I saw him then, moving fast, passing the bar and
moving south down Park. I watched him look around,
this way and that, and keep moving, almost running
now. I stayed put, another ten seconds, and then stepped
out from the wall.

Sorry, I said to the barman.

He smiled. Nothing worse than bumping into your
wife, he said.

I told Marcela everything. From the beginning. Aside
from Oki I had told no one. A scar at the hands of my
brother tainted me beyond the physical mark itself; in
the telling I was sure that some doubt would surely
linger for the listener, a hint that, in some sense, I
must have deserved it. It was a foolish idea, I knew, but
persistent. Marcela sat silently. I told it all: my parents'
affair, Orr's wife's death, the toing and froing of my
early years, Orr bringing Anna and me close and then
pushing us away. Philip's presence, the few memories
blurred, uncertain, and then the one that became them
all, a simple slash, more surprise than pain. I did not
even know what was happening at first. I told her about
moving to America, about the love and emptiness that
followed, that went on following, that I could not seem
to compensate for. Even as I spoke, for those few blunt
moments in that shitty bar, I feared sounding indulgent; but the relief, in the speaking, spread through
my whole body. I told her about bringing my father to
America a decade before, about living with him then,

blind and alert, still steeped in his God. And I told her about Philip turning up at the Met, on Friday, out of nowhere. Standing before Vermeer, looking at it like a script, like it mattered. Like an instruction. Like a crime.

So you haven't seen him since you were three years old? she asked, after I seemed to have finished.

Hadn't. Yes. Thirty-five years.

Why is he here now?

I don't know.

Perhaps he's come to apologise, she said.

Is that the sense you got?

I hardly saw him, Marcela said.

But is that the sense you got?

She said nothing.

We finished our drinks and left, both tenser now, but strangely composed. Ready. The city was loaded, the buzz that always pulsed now tuned sharper. The sun was setting; the tall apartment blocks caught the low light and threw it on to the streets below with seeming violence. We surveyed the sidewalks, but it was impossible to take account of everything, everyone. We walked to the subway in silence, her arm in mine. She offered to go home with me, but I declined her kindness.

As I arrived at my apartment my father was leaving. We passed one another on the stairs.

I'm away to pray, he said. Any requests?

Still no joy with the last ones.

They that wait upon the Lord shall renew their strength, he said; they shall mount up with wings as eagles; they shall run, and not be weary; and they shall walk, and not faint.

Yeah. I know.

What is it, son? Orr asked me. You seem bothered.

My father's blindness had opened up, he felt, as much as it closed down. He found that the alertness, the sensitivity he was forced to develop – to simple sounds, changes in atmosphere, unexpected pauses in conversation – gave him something he had not had before. It was a harsh exchange, but it was out of his hands, and he had learned to take pleasure in the deliberate exercising of these new abilities, or dispositions, as he thought of them. I was a blur to him, he joked; but the subtle shifts in my mood, the times when I was sad, or frustrated, were not so easily hidden. It was not lost on me that there was an appeal in being seen and not seen at the same time.

I held my silence, left him to it. I moved around the empty apartment, a dull threat lurking in every thought, every movement. The basic actions of life seem both enlarged and redundant. The monologue ratcheted up, deafening: What am I going to do, walk the streets in endless fear, hesitating on every corner? Who can live like that? And anyway, surely I am exaggerating everything, creating a monster where there is only a man.

When Orr returned I was already in bed. I lay there, listened to him shuffling around the living room, making himself tea, putting some music on, the volume carefully low. *If he knocks on my door I tell him now.* In ten minutes I am asleep.

*

I took two days off. Fuck the raised eyebrows. I did not
tell my father, leaving early in the morning as usual but
spending the day in cafés in the Village. I say cafés. I had
spent my fair share of the last decade in Makeen's, and
The Gattuso; had caught the eyes of enough men passing
by to satisfy a lifetime. I say eyes. Not for a few years
though. One heartbreak may be regarded as misfortune,
etc. Another story, I suppose.

I also called Anna, talked around the topic enough to
stir her frustration.

Sam, she said. Do you want to talk about Philip?

I've just been thinking about him recently, I said.

Any particular reason?

I wonder where he is, what he's doing.

I get it, Sam. I understand. But he is long gone. We
would have heard something of him, by now, one of us.
You know?

I expect you're right, I said, satisfied that she knew
nothing I didn't.

I returned to the Met, and to the safety of my desk. The
remove was a relief, but the awareness that I did not
know what was happening below, that the floors now
contained for me some menace, was almost worse. I
could barely read the words on my screen. Every couple
of minutes I walked to the window of the office and
watched people mill placidly on the steps below. Two
or three times I spotted him, and then realised it wasn't
him, and I returned to my desk, dragging, like a dead
deer over a hill, my concentration back to the present.

Day by day I wait, I expect. Day by day he does

not appear. Or rather, I don't know if he appears. I realise I am trapped; unable to move in any direction, self-enclosed.

I began, at lunchtimes, to venture out, on to the floors. I walked from gallery to gallery, anticipating, steeling myself. In the African sections downstairs I expect him to show up at any moment, to step out from behind a bust or tomb; the masks from Burkina Faso and Benin and Cameroon, as I pass them, assume his spirit. But he does not appear. Marcela checks in on me every evening, and we begin even to enjoy the subtleties of our unspoken communication, a series of nods and glances that make us feel we are accomplices. After only a few days it seems unreal, as though perhaps I really did imagine it. I play and replay the two encounters, but they shift in and out of focus, phrases assuming lives of their own. I cannot think what they actually mean.

Greenwich sucked me in again. Make of that what you will. I had left it behind, I thought, retreated to an online date or two every few months; a meal, a movie, laughter out of time. The serene benefaction of desire contained. So on, so forth. But those few visits reminded me (like I had really forgotten) of breath on my neck, skin on my skin. The danger of Philip, or whatever it was, reawakened other appetites, other vulnerabilities, and the complications of enjoyment they entailed. I believed in love as much as the next man, depending on who the next man was.

I never stayed out all night, but late enough for my

father to notice. I was there less, but I saw him more. I mean: I paid attention. The evenings I was home I sat and watched him, knowing he couldn't see me, wondering whether he thought of his son at all, his eldest. Still I said nothing. On the following Friday, after an encounter without an outcome, I arrived home just after midnight to find him awake, sitting at the table by the window, practising braille. This was a new thing for him; having resisted for so long, it was as though he had decided that he was going to live long enough after all, and so had begun, slowly but concretely, to learn the language.

You're still up? I said, going straight to the fridge.

These words are not going to learn themselves.

Do you want a beer?

It was a new thing, this drinking together. Orr had drunk rarely in Ireland. He was not teetotal exactly, but had a precise awareness of a capacity within himself – learned through watching his own father – for relentlessness. With alcohol he had always exercised caution, largely from seeing the damage – relentless damage – it had caused in numerous families he visited. Now, however, here – in his new home, his responsibilities shaken off – he allowed himself a little more freedom. He had only a beer at a time, two at the most, and – so far as I know – only with me, in the apartment.

I handed him the bottle and sat down opposite.

You're in a good mood tonight, he said.

Get thee behind me, Satan.

He smiled.

Are you getting there? I asked.

Dot by dot.

We sat in silence, sipping our beers. I put on some music.

Can I ask you something? he said. He didn't wait for me to answer. Why do you never bring a lover back?

I laughed. The alcohol, I was aware, had relaxed me. How do you know? I said.

Do you think it would bother me?

That's nothing to do with it.

It wouldn't.

I felt an anger, unspecific, rise in me. It's nothing to do with you.

He raised his hands.

We sat another minute, saying nothing. The music floated around us, a piano piece by Schoenberg. Orr began to play his fingers on the table. I watched them, trying to locate the anger, hold it in place. It kept moving.

What difference does it make to you? I said.

He stopped moving his fingers. None at all, he said. I just don't want you to think it would bother me. You can do what you want.

Of course I can do what I want. It's my fucking house. I necked the rest of my beer, walked to the fridge for another. You know nothing about me, I said to him. What do you know about your children? What was the point in even having them?

He stood up, shuffled to his room. He turned to face me. I didn't mean anything by it, Samuel, he said.

He disappeared into his room, closing the door quietly behind him. I stood where I was, by the fridge, felt my head spinning, the dull emptiness thudding. I realised how drunk I was. Schoenberg played on, a soundtrack repeating, an unravelling melody always approaching itself and then falling away. Philip returns, the man I had met – twice now – replaced by the boy, the boy who had played with me, laughed with me, tickled me. I drink quickly, then open another. I am in my mother's bedroom. I drink until Schoenberg is finished.

I woke late, almost ten; my mouth dry, wasted, my head concrete. I heard Orr in the living room; the previous night's conversation came back to me in pieces. I couldn't remember exactly what I said, but the aftertaste was bitter. I lay on my bed until I heard him go out.

I finally left the apartment, a little after midday, and walked, on a hunch, to the church. It was a small, red-brick building, settled between a cheap grocer's and a nameless glass-fronted shop offering, in tall, blunt capitals, TATTOOS REMOVED. The church's signage was smaller, but still eye-catching – IGLESIA PENTECOSTAL DE JESUS CRISTO EL LIBERTADOR – painted by hand on a blue wooden board. I tried the door, and it opened. I stepped into the small lobby, frosted glass and fake wood panelling, like the waiting area of a cheap dentist, and through another door into the sanctuary. Orr was sitting at the back. A young woman, in her early twenties at most, was dusting the chairs, moving slowly along the rows, side to side towards the front. She was laughing, presumably at something Orr had just said.

Who's that? Orr asked.

The woman looked at me. Who are you? Her accent thick, heavy.

I'm Samuel Orr, I said.

No, I'm Samuel Orr, said my father, standing up.

The woman laughed, though surely, I thought, she didn't understand. She was laughing simply to please my father. I looked at his face, and saw a pride there, a satisfaction, almost sexual.

This is my son, Ceci. Sam, this is Ceci.

She jerked her head up in acknowledgement, saying nothing.

Do you want to get some lunch, Dad?

My father shuffled towards me. Okay Ceci. Until next time. You be good.

I'm always good, señor. Maybe you be good for once, eh? She laughed.

I'm too old to be good, said Orr.

We ordered food in a Vietnamese café, huddled together at a shared table beside an old Chinese couple who ate without speaking. The slurps and clinks of their meal amused Orr, who was clearly on good form.

I'm sorry about last night, I said.

Don't worry about it.

The tiny woman who worked behind the counter brought over our sandwiches. Who is this? she said.

This is my son, Sam, said Orr.

She inclined herself slightly towards me, in what I supposed was a greeting. I attempted to return the gesture.

You look like your father.

Brilliant, I said.

Are you happy here? I asked my father, when she returned to the counter.

I like the food.

I mean in New York.

Orr took a bite, and I waited, watching him.

You haven't asked me that since about a year after I arrived, he said. He raised his hand. That's not a complaint. Just an observation. Do I like it here? Yes. I do. I like Bushwick, I like the *iglesia*, I like spending time with Guest and his kids. Sometimes I worry that I am too much in your space.

I did not answer. He went on.

I know it is different for you. That you do not have the freedom you would have if I was not here. But then I think, he said, that you would tell me. You are not a coward.

I smiled. He left the word hanging. Smart bastard.

I'm not sure you would know if I am or am not, I said finally.

The old couple beside us stood up and put on their coats. As they left, Orr shuffled along the bench, extending himself. Colonising, I thought, unwillingly.

You are not a coward, he said. Experiencing fear does not make you a coward.

You think I experience fear?

Don't we all? he said.

What are you scared of? I asked him.

He smiled, amused. Maybe I have not tasted life enough. I am nearly eighty years old.

Do you worry you might have it wrong?

Life?

God. The universe.

He laughed. What have I lost if I have? I sinned, I was forgiven.

Is it that simple?

Forgiveness is everything, he said. There is not a person I have met – anywhere, anytime, any kind of person – who would not be relieved by forgiveness. Forgiving others, forgiving themselves, being forgiven.

I don't need God for that, I said.

I do, said Orr.

We walked through Prospect Park afterwards, Orr's hand in my arm. Birds flitted overhead, their screeches mingled with kids' shouting and crying. The sun was weak, and described everything – trees, grass, the circling paths – with an impressibility, the sense that a strong enough hand could rework it. The brutal pace of the surrounding streets was temporarily substituted; it was like being in another city, a kinder city. Still I was alert, scouring the park for my inevitable brother.

We rested on a bench near the zoo. Monkey howls echoed in the distance.

I need to talk to you, I said to him.

Is that not what we're doing?

Philip is in New York.

He did not start, did not express surprise. He turned his face slowly towards me.

He showed up at the museum, I said.

When?

Two weeks ago. Three different occasions.

You didn't know he was here? He hadn't been in touch?

He just appeared.

Orr half smiled. Like a ghost, he said. What does he want?

I don't know. I told him I didn't want to speak to him. Maybe nothing.

Orr turned away from me. In the distance a dog chased a child on a bike across a piece of wasteland, the dust rising up into a sun-filled gauze. I wondered exactly what he could see of it.

There is no nothing, he said. I got a call from Magee. About a month ago.

The monkey howls sounded closer.

Magee?

The mechanic I worked with. Philip showed up there. Looking for me. Five, six weeks ago.

Did he tell him where you were?

He told him I was in New York. Living with you. But he got cautious when Philip started asking questions. Felt something was a bit off. He called me to tell me.

He didn't give him the address?

I don't think he even has it. But no, he said he only told him I was here. In the city.

Did he say why he was looking for you?

No. What did he say to you?

I told him what had happened. He listened, quietly, looking suddenly older. I wondered what pictures he returned to, how similar or different they were to mine. Forty yards behind us a fence rattled violently, and I turned to see a macaque, teeth bared, beating its fist heavily on the chain-link. I bared my teeth back and he paused for a second and then returned to his pointless struggle with more force.

I went back to the paintings. I could sit no longer at my desk, the floors beneath me teeming with the unknown. I asked Balthasar for a few days back on the floor, ostensibly for research. He raised his eyebrows but made it happen. So for a week I moved between the eighteenth and nineteenth centuries, from Goya to Courbet. It was quiet in the outer wings in the first few days; still, I was visible.

I cannot say what I wanted to happen. Did I want a confrontation? There is a pleasure in shame, is there not, albeit a vicious one; the brutal, satisfying confirmation that we are unworthy of our satisfactions. A longing took me over, for something I would even now find hard to identify. *When nothing is named, confusion grows and with it comes anguish.* The pulse thickened, my blood drawn towards the outside. It was not revenge, I swear, but it was not not revenge. How much sharper the thirst of the swimmer.

I stood alone, in front of Courbet's *Woman with a Parrot.* I had always loved the bird, the rough, bold strokes, flashes of colour. The gallery was still, silent; I briefly closed my eyes. The hand on my shoulder was a jolt, and I turned, startled. Philip lifted his hand off theatrically, but he was standing close, too close, and I took a step back, almost falling into the painting. His face was curled into a forced smile. I stepped to the side to allow me away from the wall without having to move towards him.

You weren't expecting me? he said. Sorry for my absence, the world makes its demands. But now I need your help. I want to see my father.

His hand twitched, and he tapped the ground nervously with the heel of his right foot. His eyes were clear, though, precise.

What for? I asked.

You must believe me.

What must I believe?

I need to see him.

He's an old man, I said. He has had enough. A thought came to me. You know he's blind?

He was blind long before his eyes went, he said drily. He owes me. Or I owe him. Either way.

Owes you what?

He shook his head, as at an infuriating child. Nothing is free, he said. Everything must be paid for.

There was no smile, no irony; even the indulgence of self-righteousness was absent. He looked, in truth, pained, his face contracted. His hands moved imperceptibly, as though he was channelling all his energy into stopping them shaking. I thought, for a moment, that he was about to cry.

This is ridiculous, I said. I'm not having this conversation. I moved to walk away.

He reached out and grabbed my arm. I attempted to shake it off, but he held firm.

Justice, he said.

I stared at him.

He repeated: Justice.

With my free hand I pointed to my face.

A Korean family walked into the gallery. The son, six or seven years old, stared at us. I composed myself, again began to walk away, but he held my arm tight, would not let go. The father of the boy, younger than both Philip and I, saw what was happening. Philip stared at him, and he said nothing, taking his son's hand and walking him, with his wife and daughter, quickly into the next gallery.

He let go. I was young, Sam. I am sorry. You have nothing to fear from me.

And my father? Your father?

He shook his head.

Go home, I said.

Don't misunderstand me, Sam. I am not asking, I am telling.

I turned and began to stride towards the door.

Do not walk away from me, Sam.

I kept walking, towards the adjoining gallery. I am almost through the gap when I hear the sound, the tear. I turn to see Philip walk in the opposite direction, dropping something into his pocket. Courbet's painting is sliced neatly down the middle, a clean, brutal cut. The woman, lying back, is in two pieces, a magician's trick gone wrong. Her smile, now that the canvas hangs sagging, appears more like a rictus of pain, the parrot staring at her in disbelief.

The museum director was a man in his late fifties called Rollins. He was trim, precise; he had an easy authority. I'd always liked him. Beside him was a younger woman – the head of human resources, called Carzola, who I didn't really know – and two other men who were introduced and whose names I immediately forgot. I sat across the table from them, and beside me Balthasar, nervously moving his hands in and out of each other like koi in a pond. He kept looking to me then away again, a disappointed parent.

I was not nervous. This surprised me. I had settled into what happened as though it were a kind of fate, as though it were somehow predestined. I was aware that this thought brought me, with some irony, into what I imagined was my father's world-view: Moirai, effect, the mysterious workings of God. As the thought played itself out, I was struck that I had it wrong. Orr did not seem tied to a fixed universe.

Rollins passed a sheet of paper across the desk. On it was a description of what had happened the previous day. Read this and tell me if there's anything you contest, he said.

I lifted the paper and read. No one spoke. After two minutes I handed it back.

Close enough, I said.

You told us yesterday that the man was your brother, Rollins said.

Half-brother, I interrupted.

Half-brother? Carzola repeated.

We have the same father.

And you had seen him previously in the museum?

Three times before yesterday, yes.

And outside the museum?

No. Before he turned up a couple of weeks ago I hadn't seen him in thirty-five years.

You had an argument, Rollins said.

Yes.

What was it about?

It's hard to say.

Samuel, I'm not sure if you're aware of how serious this is.

I am aware.

Carzola leaned forward. It is important that you tell us everything. Your brother destroyed a Courbet, worth many millions of dollars . . .

Half-brother, I said.

This drew a smile from Rollins. Half-smile. What kind of relationship do you have with your half-brother? he asked.

I pointed to my face. I watched Rollins take it in. There was a surprising satisfaction in his horror. Carzola had not understood. What do you mean? she asked.

He gave me this, I said. When I was three years old. That was the last time I saw him.

The man at the end of the table, who until this point had been silent, spoke. Are you in danger?

I felt it again, that distilled shock that had haunted my childhood, a memory fighting its way to the surface.

I don't believe so. I don't know.

Rollins nodded. Okay, Sam. Thanks for your time. There is a procedure we have to go through, an investigation. In the short term you'll be put on paid leave.

What will happen to the painting? I asked.

It will be fixed, Rollins said. As though it never happened.

*

Orr inclined his head, a smile, rueful. Justice, he repeated, chewing over the word like a piece of food. I am telling him, again, what I said to Philip, what he said to me. We are back in the sandwich shop, escaping the claustrophobia of the apartment. Safety in numbers.

And then he sliced the painting?

I had turned and walked away. He'd already tried to stop me twice. Why do you want me to go through this again?

Orr shook his head, dismissing my protest. Humour me, he said.

Yes, and then I heard the canvas tear and turned back and he was walking away.

You didn't tell me what painting it was.

It was a Courbet. *Woman with a Parrot.*

Of a woman?

With a parrot, yes.

What is she doing with the parrot?

She's just lying there. It's perched on her hand.

Is she naked?

Yes.

Is she beautiful?

What do you mean?

You work in an art gallery and don't know what beautiful is?

It's a museum. And yes I do.

Well is she beautiful?

I suppose she is.

He eats his sandwich with evident satisfaction.

Describe her to me, he says.

I'd need to be looking at it.

So look at it.

I picked up my mobile but set it down immediately.

She's lying on her back, I said, a kind of awkward angle. She's in a room but it almost feels like a tent because of the way the curtain is pulled back. Outside there are these dark, green trees, and just a small amount of sky, turning orange. There's a light from above, somewhere in the room you can't see. It's falling on her, making her skin soft, this beautiful cream-white colour. Her curves are beautiful too. Her breasts are there, obviously, but you actually notice her belly more, a sort of tiny mound, a roundness. And her thighs are thick, powerful. Her hair is splayed out on the white sheet she's lying on, going in all directions, thick brown wavy hair, lighter at the ends. And she has one arm stretched up, where the parrot is perched, looking down at her.

Orr sat transfixed, eyes shut firmly to the world. I stopped talking and watched him, his breathing, his body pushing the air in and out, inside him somewhere this picture I had been building. I wondered again at what he saw, what Courbet's painting looked like to a man who had never seen it, who had heard only my rough description.

It's beautiful, he said.

Yes.

And they can fix it?

So they say.

We sat a little longer. I finished eating, watched the other customers. Orr seemed briefly lost in a world of his own.

I broke into his silence. What do you think he wants?

Violence, he said. Well. He thinks he wants violence. But it's not violence he wants. He wants something else. He thinks violence will give it to him.

What does he want?

What everybody wants, he said. Peace.

For a week I was at home. My father and I circled one another, rarely in the same room. A dull tension crept in, something undefined pulling at us, injecting a sharpness into our interactions. It was as though, I sensed, by telling him what Philip had said and done, I had acted as his representative. I felt Orr's eyes follow me around the apartment, aware that my blurred outline was, to him, no different from any other.

I could not shake Philip as I walked the streets, every alleyway hiding him, every corner an opening. It did not matter that he did not appear, he was inside me. It was an unexpected relief to return to work; the Met now, thanks to the increased security, the one place I felt at least marginally safe. The guards regarded me cautiously, though none mentioned the incident directly. I checked in with Balthasar every day, to hear if anything unusual had happened.

On my third day back I was called in to see Rollins. I sat opposite him. He held up a letter.

This arrived, addressed to you, he said. Do you mind if I open it?

Go ahead, I said.

He pulled out a piece of paper:

O lord, thou hast searched me, and known me. Thou knowest my downsitting and mine uprising, thou understandest my thought afar off. Thou compassest my path and my lying down, and art acquainted with all my ways. For there is not a word in my tongue, but, lo, O Lord, thou knowest it altogether. Thou hast beset me behind and before, and laid thine hand upon me. Such knowledge is too wonderful for me; it is high, I cannot attain unto it. Whither shall I go from thy spirit? or whither shall I flee from thy presence? If I ascend up into heaven, thou art there: if I make my bed in hell, behold, thou art there. If I take the wings of the morning, and dwell in the uttermost parts of the sea; Even there shall thy hand lead me, and thy right hand shall hold me. If I say, Surely the darkness shall cover me; even the night shall be light about me. Yea, the darkness hideth not from thee; but the night shineth as the day: the darkness and the light are both alike to thee. For thou hast possessed my reins: thou hast covered me in my mother's womb.

There was no name. The handwriting was neat, precise.

This is your brother?

I would guess so.

Does it mean anything to you?

Not specifically.

I have a duty to look after the museum, he said.

I nodded. I felt sorry for him.

I went back to the floor, wandered the long rooms stared at by the paintings. It seems strange to insist upon it, but I was calm. I did not know around which corner

Philip would appear, but I knew he would, eventually, and when he did I believed I would be ready for him. A sense of destiny settled in me, and even the memory of Anna's scepticism was not enough to drown it out.

I did not have to wait long. A few days later I was walking through Bushwick, coming home from a friend's house, and I spotted him. He was almost a block away, walking, it appeared, without particular intention. He took a right, walked down Harman as far as Evergreen. As he walked he glanced around him, looking up at the apartments on either side. At Evergreen he took a left, then another left at Greene, walking back towards the main road. He was scouring. He did not know – not yet, at any rate – but he had the neighbourhood. I lived a good half-mile away. I got there quickly, but my father was absent. I ran down to the church. As I arrived congregants were leaving; I saw my father towards the back, laughing with a young black man. I pushed through the rest of them – most of them knew me by now and nodded or smiled – and took him by the arm.

Dad, we need to go.

He was effusive; his pride of me at its greatest among his fellow worshippers. Samuel, he said, calm yourself.

Philip's here, I said.

He was caught between maintaining his easy charm with the young man at his side, and something else; not fear. Maybe anticipation.

Here?

Nearby. Looking, hunting. We need to go.

The young man stared at us. Are you okay? he enquired, gently but with unconcealed excitement, sensing scandal.

Orr excused himself and I guided him away from the church, whispers already at our backs. It was getting dark, the air chilling. We walked quickly. I told him what I had seen. He said nothing, allowed me to lead him.

Inside the apartment he sat down at the table. I was exasperated; he appeared unfazed.

So what now? I said.

I don't know, son. To every thing there is a season.

That doesn't help.

What do you want to do? he asked.

You can't stay here.

I saw him weigh me up. I saw him measure his objections, then hold them.

He is around here somewhere, looking for us, I said.

It will be okay.

How do you know? It's a matter of time. Today, tomorrow. He will find us. Then what? It's a matter of time.

Everything is a matter of time.

You're a fool, I said.

Fear and shame.

What?

Fear and shame, he repeated. Almost everything we do is out of fear and shame. All of us. I do not want for you and I to live like that. Philip must be Philip. You and I must be you and I.

I called Guest, who called his grandson in Queens, Zico. He and his wife agreed to put my father up for a few

days. We took a taxi around midnight, and I got him
settled, thanked them for their kindness. They seemed
bemused. By the time I got home it was almost two in
the morning. I went to bed but lay awake, my body
pulsing; the sight of Philip walking in front of me –
leading me, I began to imagine – forced itself into the
space where sleep should have been. I got up, opened
a beer. I stared at the street below, almost willing him
to appear. How dedicated was he, how far would he
go? I felt again that appetite, that unnameable hunger.
I returned to bed and fell asleep, eventually, and woke
at six with the image of my mother, younger, attending Philip's scar. She is close to his face, he can feel her
breath, smell her skin, see the moist glisten of sweat
on her shoulderblade. Except it is not Philip, it is Orr.
Except it is not Orr, it is me.

The following evening, I went to a bar in the Village.
Let's leave it anonymous. I used to go there for sex, years
ago, so much easier to find than love, and less expen-
sive. Anyway, I knew this bar, I knew the men who
frequented it. The type of men. It was not as clean as the
others; the hangers-on all hung on a little more, if you
know what I mean. I nursed a drink, watching the room
just like everyone else. One or two men nodded towards
me; I waved them away. Eventually I was approached
by someone who looked like they might do. His hair
was greasy, and he repeatedly, as he offered me a drink,
tucked it behind his ears. His skin was pock-marked,
darker on one side of his face than the other. His eyes
were bright though, clear, too clear. Tripped up, high.

He spoke slowly, deliberately, as though to a foreigner. None of this was important. It was the marks on his knuckles that appealed.

We went to the bathrooms and I tried to fuck him. I knew already that he wouldn't let me, but I saw how far I could push him, how much he had in him, where the line was. I was good at this, at least. When I had his measure – just before he beat the living shit out of me – I stopped, and sat on the floor.

Do you want to make some money? I asked him.

This is not . . . he said. I am not . . .

Not for this, I said. I need you to hurt somebody.

I stepped out of the entrance to my apartment. I walked, slowly, down the street. I paused halfway along, punched at my phone. I smiled, laughed, as though having received a humorous message. A group of teenagers swam past me, around me, parting then re-forming, their shrill voices ringing in their wake. I was invisible to them. There are none so blind as those who will not see.

It was late, after eleven. My friend – I shall resist naming him too – had not told me where he would be standing, so I would be less inclined to look for him. Nonchalance as weapon. I dropped my phone back into my pocket. My heart hammered in my chest, but I steadied myself. This was the third time we had tried this. It was no more likely to work this time than the others, but there persisted an unmistakable thrill, a charge. I walked to the end of the street, turned right towards the park a quarter-mile away. Much of Bushwick had been prettified; but not this part. Drunks and users stalked it at night, looking for fixes. Half the lights were broken. Scattered glass flecked the path. I sat down on a bench, took out my mobile, feigned attention. I waited.

After ten minutes I became aware of being watched. I mean, in this park you were always watched, but it was a specific kind of attention, directed. I knew it was him. After five minutes he stepped forward, towards me. The sick, pale light caught his scar, rendered it even more garish. He nodded, as though a friendly greeting.

I stared at him. It was a strange moment; the hatred I expected did not materialise. I felt something closer to curiosity, almost empathy. Though I knew what was coming. From behind him, out of the darkness – very *noir*, I know – appeared my friend. Philip glanced over his shoulder to where I was looking, realising too late. The first punch hit him clean; a crunch, a kind of echoey thud, and he dropped. I stood up and moved away while further punches were delivered. It was not like the films, I was thinking. The sounds were less full, more muffled. I looked around the park but if there were other people there they were wise enough to pay no attention. I heard the report of a bone breaking (arm? collar? rib?) and Philip cried out, more whimper than scream. I told my friend to stop. He didn't stop. He kicked Philip in the stomach now, now the face. Stop, I said louder, and he looked at me, and swung his foot again, his heel this time landing on the side of Philip's face. I heard myself shouting now. Fucking stop. Money? I shouted, money?, but still he ignored me. I hurled myself towards him, and as I arrived I felt my own face caught by his fist. The pain was sudden, intuitive, but I was on my feet again in a second and forced my shoulder, low and hard, into his midriff. He fell back. I was on my knees, staring at him. He glared back, breathing heavily; returned, it seemed, to sense. I threw money at him – I'm not even sure how much – and he picked it off the ground, climbing to his feet. He smiled at me, and walked nonchalantly away.

I turned around. Philip was lying prone, one arm splayed awkwardly above his head, a fictional victim. I got close enough to hear him breathing, but he didn't respond when I spoke to him, tapped his face. I hid my number, dialled an ambulance. I got slowly, painfully, to my feet. I watched him. One minute, two. In the moment I cannot say what I feel because I do not know. I saw a figure at the far end of the park, a woman, sway-ing, apparently drunk, looking towards us. I walked out of the park, along the cycle lane. There was a dive bar open on the corner. I stepped inside, ordered a whisky, and sipped silently until I heard the sirens.

I slept like a child.

I wasted two days before going to the hospital. Waited. Freudian autocorrect. I called first, told them I was a work colleague. They outlined visiting regulations and explained that he would not be released any time soon. He had had a haemorrhage in his chest – a blunt trauma, they said – and, whilst he was stable, he was not yet out of the woods. I hung up and searched 'blunt trauma': *This happens when a body part collides with something else, usually at high speed. Blood vessels inside the body are torn or crushed either by shear forces or a blunt object. Examples are car accidents, physical assaults, and falls.*

After work I took the subway downtown to Mount Sinai Hospital – *honour thy father and thy mother* – and made my way to the ward. It was a small, personal room at the end of a long corridor. I steeled myself; I still felt blank, impassive, but something rattled in me, ice in a glass: a mute awareness of deception. I looked through the small window and saw a girl sitting beside the bed. She was fifteen, sixteen; dark-haired, pale. Her back was mostly to me, so I could not clearly make out her features, except when she shifted position. For some reason she put me in mind of a Velázquez. She was leaning towards him, talking. His eyes were closed. I couldn't tell if he was asleep. There seemed to be, in the carry of her shoulders, her delivery – I could not, of course, hear what she was saying – something more of complaint than story. An exasperation.

The corridor behind me was empty, silent. I felt – bluntly – like an intruder. After a few minutes she turned, as though suddenly aware of my presence. She stared at me – my face framed inside the tiny window – and turned back to Philip. I was well dressed, of course. I suppose to her I looked like a doctor.

I went downstairs, drank a coffee. I considered leaving – What am I here for anyway? – but forced myself back an hour later. I looked through the small window: the girl was gone. A small hesitation and then I was in the room, standing beside his bed, staring down at him. He was asleep, or appeared to be. I stared at him without – strike me down etc. – remorse. His face was bruised; dark patches gave way to a sickly spreading yellow. His mouth had been reset; I saw the marks of the wires on his neck. It was strange to stand in front of him like this, above him. Fear absent, and pity. But so too hatred, anger. My eyes searched his face, his body, as though for clues; something to hang myself on. The past, where I had lived for ever, opened up into the present. It felt like the lines between these were no longer relevant, no longer existed.

I saw myself reach out and touch him. I pulled back hair from his forehead, and moved the back of my fingers down his cheek. His breathing did not change. I set my hand, palm flat, on his chest. His heart: thump, thump, thump. We have been here before. Haven't we? I press down a little. Testing. He does not flinch. I wonder if he has slipped into a coma. I lean my head down above his, turn my ear to his mouth. His breath comes in short, sharp draws. No, then. It is warm against me. I feel it enter my ear, travel inside, to where? I stand up again, again stare at him. My hand moves to his chest, up to his neck. His skin is clammy, tight; a thin film of moisture. My hand rests on his throat. I feel the pulse through it, his life pressing back. It is too easy, I think, but my fingers find such easy purchase. I am a longing I cannot say. I feel my arm stiffen, tighten, as though he is resisting. I move my face to his, closer and closer. Still his eyes are shut, still his breath, barely. I lean my face to his, my lips to his lips, and I kiss him.

I do not know for how long this happens. I move back, take my hand away. I feel my own heart, but it is barely beating. I stand in the middle of the room, a little away from the bed, a supplicant. The hum of the equipment suddenly seems deafening. His eyes remain closed, the landscape of his face unmoved. I am convinced, somehow, that a transaction has taken place.

I returned the following day. I do not know exactly why. There is something to be said for presence. I walked along the corridor towards his room; from behind me I heard a shout. I turned to see the girl. She moved towards me, quickly.

You fucking asshole, she said.

She looked different at this angle, this distance. Less Velázquez, more Goya. Her eyes were tiny black balls, penetrating, direct. Her features seemed somehow undefined, as though she was still growing into them, finding their edges. I suppose she was. No more than sixteen. I knew too, with certainty, that Philip was her father.

She reached me and pushed me hard, in the chest. I stumbled backwards, stayed on my feet.

Who are you? she asked.

She went to push me again; I put my arms up.

Who are you? she repeated, louder. I saw her see it, the scar. An infinitesimal flinch, a calculation.

I'm a friend, I said, stupidly.

She stared at me, hatred pushing at her speech. Bullshit. You brought them. She flickered in the air, her taut movement shimmering, her body a vibration.

Brought who? I said.

She paused, measuring me. Her narrow eyes narrowed.

Who? I said again. She looked towards Philip's room. I turned towards it, took a step.

He's not there, she said. They took him away.

I turned to her. Who?

The police. She was retreating from the anger, beginning to believe me.

When?

Who are you? she asked again.

So I told her.

I picked my father up the same evening. As I helped him into the cab, Zico pulled me aside, smiling.

He is some piece of work, your father.

I raised my eyebrows.

You know a young woman came every day? For an hour. Ceci. She would rub his feet, listen to him talk. He is teaching her about music. So he says. It is okay, it was not a problem. I hope I have that when I am his age.

I shook Zico's hand, climbed in beside my father, smiling. We sat in silence as the cab snaked its way through Queens, down into Brooklyn. The bland, grey streets seemed transformed, illuminated. Rescued. I was aware of the foolishness of the thought, but it rooted in me regardless.

Before we got through the door of the apartment, Orr tightened his grip. Tell me what happened, son.

He was unsurprised by it, by all of it, it seemed. I had told Sarah almost everything; but I spared him nothing. We had come this far together, what harm a little further? It was true: I found myself wanting something from him. A word, a sign. Do we ever grow up?

Tell me more about her, he said.

I described her as best I could, her sharp wit and hot blood, but really I did not know. She lives with her grandmother in Fordham, I said. Her mother died, a few years ago. Philip did not cope. The more I talked the more I wondered myself.

I would like to meet her, he said. What's her name?

I can't believe I haven't told him. Of course I can. Sarah, I said.

She had given me her number, but for two days my messages went unanswered. I stared at my phone for what felt like hours at a time, but it lay on my desk unresponsive. I examined my own texts – had I been too forceful, too insipid, too quick or slow? – like a teenager myself, I couldn't help thinking. At home in the evening my father stalked, manhandling his way around my apartment like a blind Humboldt. Our interactions were minimal; each of us awaiting an announcement, an invitation we could not conjure.

On the third day it arrived. Short, direct, straightforward – **Come for dinner, Sarah** – and an address. She lived near the train station, and my father, ever the democrat, insisted we take the train. To prepare ourselves, he said, as though the New Haven line were a pilgrimage.

I do not recall ever being as nervous as standing on the steps of the house, a two-storey grey-clad working-class Connecticut affair, basic as they come. Paint peeled off at the edges; a dull grey stain spread from below the guttering on the right, like a disease. The street itself was quiet of traffic, though Mexican music blared from somewhere nearby. My father stood beside me as we waited, immaculate in a suit, seemingly unfazed. I stared at him, as much to distract myself as anything else, and he reached out and took my hand, as though I were a child again, and I was flooded with both gratitude and anger. I almost jumped when the door finally opened and there stood Sarah, looking first at me but then ignoring me entirely, turning her attention to Orr, my father, her grandfather, who looked up towards her and said – I'm not sure whether ironically or not, as though it were his door she had just opened – Welcome.

She sat us down at the dining table and began immediately to carry in bowls of food from the kitchen, refusing my help.

Where is your grandmother? I asked, and she shrugged, and I realised, suddenly, that she had done all this herself. So many more questions came, I had to stop myself. My anxiety was palpable, running through me. I could feel Orr's blind eyes boring, his head shaking almost imperceptibly from side to side. Calm yourself, Sam, I imagined him saying, and I did.

She was reserved but not intimidated. Orr, typically, bypassed small-talk, his curiosity unswerving as a child's. In a similar spirit she answered his questions directly: where she'd grown up, why she lived with her grandmother, what happened to her mother (hit by a truck, she said, three years ago, while crossing a road in Portchester; Orr didn't flinch). She began to lose interest when I interjected with questions of school, of her future plans. Her answers dropped to a word or phrase, her shoulders hunching into apathy. I felt guilt for occupying the space my father, in his bluntness, had created.

As she carried the plates into the kitchen the front door rattled open and a woman appeared, in her late sixties, hair grey and unkempt, her teeth stained from smoking. As she entered the room she was rummaging in her bag, and stuck a cigarette in her mouth as she looked up. She started as she saw us, but immediately moved on past, staring at us all the while, into the kitchen. I looked at my father, whispered quietly that it must be her grandmother. He nodded. We sat in silence as they spoke in hushed tones in the kitchen, a quiver in Sarah's voice, pained and plaintive.

A few seconds later Sarah appeared with bowls of ice cream. Her face drawn, an edge in her movements. My insights are few, but I know shame when I see it, and it was as painful to me as if it had been my own body. She sat down opposite us again, silently, once or twice looking towards the kitchen, her grandmother's unseen presence everything. I felt for her, I really did, but was dumb to help, my awkwardness, I well knew, just an addendum to her own. Orr leaned across and took my arm, helping himself to his feet. I moved to stand up, to help him, but he nudged me back into my seat.

We both watched him as he edged his way around the table, to the empty doorframe. He stepped inside, and we heard him say, Hello, I'm Samuel Orr. Is there a seat you could help me into?

*

Sarah and I sat across from one another. We ate without speaking, listening instead to the muffled voices in the kitchen, the exclamations, the – unexpected, I sensed – laughter. I watched Sarah slowly let her shoulders out, the tension releasing. Her eyes gave themselves to tears, but the rest of her face was impassive, and when I went to speak she snapped her fingers together sharply to shut me up. I smiled, laughed – I couldn't help it – at the excess of the gesture, and then she smiled too, and her face, with a thin wet line down either cheek, was suddenly alive, transfigured. She let herself breathe, breaths that came and went like a child after running, taking in and letting out as much as she could.

A few days later she messaged to say she was going to visit her father. He had eschewed representation and his case had been heard quickly, without our knowledge. For 'criminal damage', a term Courbet himself would have appreciated, he received a three-year sentence with a one-year minimum, to be served in a holding centre thirty miles north of the city. It was a week before he could get out of bed, but he was now able to receive visitors.

I warned her that Philip may not now want to see us. I had, as I said, told her who I was, but in every story there are gaps, and I'd been careful enough, or cowardly enough, to leave out some of the darker ingredients. Even as she and my father exchanged confidences over dinner I had seen in him a caution, a withholding, which may have been either generosity or self-protection. Still, she asked if we would come, and I realised it was for her and not for him she was asking.

I spoke to Rollins at the museum. He knew, obviously, but it was better that he knew that I knew he knew. I took the day off, hired a car. My father and I picked Sarah up in the morning. Orr sat in the front, beside me, staring ahead. For the first time in a long time he seemed nervous. The confidence sucked out of him, he sat in gloomy silence. Sarah climbed into the back, her earphones in, and I wondered if this was how it was going to go, but suddenly she took them out, synced her phone to my stereo, and filled the car with expletive-fuelled hip-hop. Orr began to tap the roof of the car with his hand, and she laughed, and we drove north.

The walls of the prison – it was a prison, whatever other words they used – were the colour of dirty water. A reek of ammonia punched at us as we walked into the reception. The woman sitting behind the desk pointed us unspeaking towards a corridor, at the end of which we entered a large, open room with tables and chairs set out like a school cafeteria. A few other inmates sat at tables across from partners, parents, children. Those who were talking at all talked quietly, pointless secrets shared.

Describe it, Orr said.

You don't want to know, I said.

We sat down and waited. None of us spoke. Regret rose up in me. What was I thinking, agreeing to this, bringing them here? Orr shuffled in his seat, his dark glasses catching the fluorescents and throwing them back. Sarah put her earphones in. I remembered, at this moment, my mother telling me – I must have been twelve or thirteen years old at the most – that in the concentration camps they had prisons. Nowhere low enough that you can't go lower.

We looked up in unison, the three of us, as the door opened. He walked into the room, looked around. It seemed to take a moment for his eyes to adjust, and then. His face moved back, a bad actor expressing surprise. He stood still, unmoved, staring at us, for ten, fifteen seconds. I reached across, took my father's hand. He walked towards us. I lifted my father out of his seat, and stood beside him. Between him and Philip.

When he reached us he faltered, put a hand on the table. His face had cleared up decently, the bruising almost gone. A few marks still darkened his forehead, and one of his eyes was bloodshot. I realised I hadn't seen his eyes before; each time I had seen him I avoided looking. They were unmistakably Orr's. I reached out my hand, but he held his own up as though in warning, and Sarah came around me and helped him into a seat.

Orr was silent throughout this interaction. He was looking at Philip, or looking at where Philip was, but his face betrayed nothing. We all sat down, Sarah beside her father, Orr and I on the other side of the table.

How are you, son? Orr said.

It sounded cruel, that *son* – though surely it wasn't. Philip rocked back and forth a little.

Did she tell you how she died? Philip said.

Who? I asked.

Philip continued to rock, forward and backward, concentrated. Sarah reached out her hand and gently put it on his back. He shook it off roughly, glared at her, and then looked back quickly at us, grimacing. The hatred was material, flesh and bone. He lifted a fist to his mouth, the knuckles pulsing white, set it back on the table.

He turned to Sarah. Did you tell them how she died? Sarah nodded.

She was knocked down, he said. She was knocked down by a truck. He stared at Orr. She was knocked down by a truck.

Orr reached out his hand, blindly, across the table. Philip jerked back, as though under attack. He shook his head, ferocious.

She was knocked down by a truck, he repeated.

I am sorry, son, Orr said, and Philip leaned forward, into his face.

You fucking should be, he said.

I pushed my hand into his chest. Such little force required. He settled back, started coughing.

Sarah stood up, walked out of the room. I wanted to follow her but could not leave my father alone.

What is this for? I said.

He lifted one hand to his face, to his scar. His face a mess of contortions, fraught and unspecific. He looked at Orr, steadily, and the movement began to slow, his face recomposing itself. He said nothing, but the rocking stopped, the shaking in the hands. His breathing steadied into a simple rise, fall. He sat, quiet, calm even, staring at my father. At his father. Two, three minutes passed. No one broke the silence.

Finally, Okay. He said okay. He stood up. My father followed the blurred form, and tried to stand up himself, awkwardly. I quickly moved to help him. Philip turned to walk away.

Wait, son, Orr said. Philip.

Philip stopped, turned.

Can I touch you? Orr said.

Philip stared at him. I see the boy again, sixteen years old, all the love and hatred packed tight into such a small space. I see him make a decision and refuse it, and then again, and then again. And then he said, Yes.

Orr moved towards him, his hands out, and found his face. My own slow heart beats beats beats. Orr's hands move across his features: his eyes, his mouth, his cheeks. He brings pressure to bear, draws Philip down towards him, and Philip allows it. Orr begins to kiss his face; forehead first, one cheek, then the other. His mouth finds the scar – even blind, he remembers – and stays with it, on it. Philip does not breathe, does not move. Eventually Orr lets go, steps back. He turns, holding out his arm for me to help him. I take it and he leads me away.

In the reception we find Sarah. I hand my father to her, and excuse myself. I find the toilets. I stare in the mirror and start to feel that my scar is moving, growing rather, expanding. I literally lift my hand to my face to stop it, and then stop myself. But still it grows. It does not actually change – I'm not seeing things, my face is as it always has been – but the sensation is pure, intimate, and a kind of liquid pain, a pleasure, rips through me. It's like a shudder: my body shakes but doesn't move. But I stand there, through it, and let it happen. I keep staring, the mirror throwing me back to myself, and it slowly subsides, water draining through rice, and I am sparkling – I honestly don't know how else to put it – and

I love myself. It is absurd, I know. I feel like I've found something I hadn't lost. It's not the quick physical ecstasy of drugs, but something slower, more – really? – sexual. I don't know.

I stared into the sink, head lowered for a full minute, maybe longer, and then looked up again. Nothing was different, nothing. And yet, and yet. I walked back into the room, and there he was, sitting alone at the table. And this time it all came, all at once. The failure of feeling before is transformed, melted down and golden-calfed. All hatred and all love; the untainted joy, the sheer crude aliveness of it. One tiny decision piled upon another, one meaning giving way to another. The sky outside is inside. The walls are arbitrary, the tables are arbitrary, blood is arbitrary. Fuck lines, fuck borders. Fuck family, fuck the law. Fuck one thing following another. Fuck the past, fuck the future. Fuck apology and disappointment. Fuck fear and shame.

I walk towards him. He looks up when he sees me approach, stares cautiously. I move to him, drag him out of his chair and embrace him. I put my lips on his cheek – that cheek, yes – and kiss him. He resists and then does not resist. When I release him I realise I am crying, but it doesn't matter.

The year found its own shape. Like any year, but not. Sarah slowly loosened, her caution attenuated. A couple of weeks after the prison visit she came to the city and I showed her around the Met, her and my father both,

feigning and not feigning interest, and then we ate
Brazilian food in a small café on 45th. I watched as the
two of them fell into one another's jokes, a shared disregard for the niceties of language pulling them closer
together. At one point she reached across and moved his
fork so that when he went to pick it up again he couldn't
find it. She laughed out loud at his confusion, and then
took his hand and guided him. I could not quite bear the
sentimentalism I felt, the joy at the pleasure they found in
each other; unwarranted, unexpected. A fortnight later
we returned to the prison, Philip sitting across from us
again, though this time in silence, tempered, but present.

And so it went – month by month the visit north, the
ice caps melting, small gestures, uncountable kindnesses
adding up to so little and so much. And in between –
at first every couple of weeks, then every week, then
every few days – Sarah's life became enmeshed with my
father's, with my own; her concerns became ours, her
joys framing and widening the joys we found possible
for ourselves. The absurdity of it all: we became a family.

For my father, I cannot say exactly how it was so easy.
Whatever measure of hesitation he carried with regard
to Philip seemed utterly irrelevant to Sarah, their ease
childlike, their connection simple. For me, it was different. Sarah got at me, into me. She refused me apathy;
she offered me – forced on me – the judgement of foolishness. She saw my failure to step fully into my life and,
unlike everyone else, did not ignore it but poked at it,
jabbed and shoved and won reactions. The complicated
magnanimity of youth. She expected as much from me
as she did from herself, and her demand was a form of

generosity. It allowed me to imagine myself at the scale, with the imagination, that she did. Expectation creating hope. With the possibility of getting lost comes the possibility of being found.

Twelve months later, we drove north again. Three of us going, four of us to return. The tension was true, but no truer than a new anticipation, a longing for possibility. We had not talked, between us, of what would happen. Philip, when he told us the day of his release, had said only that he would go home, to New Haven, Connecticut, and from there he would see. He agreed, reluctantly, to our coming for him. I had watched him more than spoken to him over these months, watched his body fight to allow him to speak, the simple descriptions even of his days a tiny battle. We were quiet in the car; I streamed Tavener to calm my nerves, and it mingled surreally with the concrete drone of the tyres on the road, the endless traffic flooding around us, drawing us forward.

We pulled in to the car park shortly after 11 a.m. We walked together, still barely speaking, each of us, I suppose, lost in our own expectations, our own fears. Sarah carried a backpack for her father's things; she looked like a misplaced hiker. The woman behind the desk – we knew her now as Marian – narrowed her eyes as we approached. She turned around, beckoned over a colleague, a man we didn't know.

Hello, Marian, I said.

Sam.

How are you?

Sam, what are you doing here?

We're here for Philip.

She looked up at her colleague. He smiled, whistled, shook his head. Philip's gone, he said. He was released yesterday. He stared at our stupid faces. He's gone, brother, he repeated.

I am back in Mount Sinai. My father is almost eighty-one years old, but will not see eighty-two. I walked here this morning, across the bridge, into Manhattan. In a couple of hours Sarah will be here too, when she finishes classes. For the last two weeks we have both come every day, at least for a short visit.

The cancer will kill him before his mind goes. Small mercies, he says, unironically. He is not in pain, but enjoys the morphine anyway. Never one to turn down pleasure where it's going. He has a steady stream of visitors. In small groups they arrive in from Bushwick and Queens, carrying various absurd gifts to impress or humour him. Guest's grandkids brought a mobile speaker loaded with hip-hop, with which he has enjoyed winding up the nurses. Ceci has come every day and stroked his face for half an hour. Even after a lifetime, I have not entirely abandoned my jealousy.

As I sit here nursing my coffee I am remembering a trip we took, last summer, before he became ill. We went to the Blue Ridge Mountains in Virginia. Sarah and I hiked a little, but mostly we just drove around, the three of us, stopping for snacks or drinks at various lookout points, the mountains green and lush stretching far in every direction. Sunsets came like gifts, and Sarah tried to adequately describe them for Orr, who seemed to take as much delight in her failure as he would have in seeing the sunsets themselves. On one day the clouds were so low we spent most of the day above them, as though out of the world entirely, looking down like gods. We pulled in at a rest stop, and Orr told a story I had not heard before. He and Anna had taken me on a day trip – I was no more than a year old – and we had gone to the Mourne Mountains. They took turns carrying me, strapped to each of their bodies in turn. We had not walked far, he told Sarah, just up the side of a hill. In the distance was Silent Valley, and a crucible of mountains surrounded us, sloping in all directions. I pointed things out to Sam, he went on, birds overhead, or the trees in the foreground, on the slope of one of the mountains. And he would stare in a sort of vague wonder. And I became aware that we were not seeing the same things. I mean, what we were both seeing were just impressions, bits of colour, shape and form, outlines, that I gave names to. When I said *trees* I wasn't really seeing trees, he said, I was seeing this clump of colour that I knew, that fitted my idea of trees. And Sam, who then didn't know the word tree, even though he experienced the same thing, saw something different, unclouded by the definition, by knowledge or expectation. I've never forgotten that strange sensation, the realisation that seeing was not just what your eyes do. Not just the light but what you do with the light, what stories you can make out of it. If you don't have useful words, or good stories, then you see less.

The world isn't just there to be seen, but to be created. When we look at the world we create it.

When Sarah gets here I will step outside, wander the streets for a while. It was, at first, just to stretch my legs, to give Sarah some time alone with her grandfather. But it is more now. A week ago, I saw him, or thought I saw him. Lurking in a doorway across 85th, only a few blocks from the museum. I cannot be sure, of course. When we look at the world we create it. But I cannot help myself, or I do not wish, perhaps, to help myself. There is no fear in my suspicion. I walk the streets now as a target, like a deer waiting to be spotted. I want to draw him into the open, to show him I have nothing to hide, that he too has nothing to fear from me. *Each being is distinct from all others*, wrote Bataille. *His birth, his death, the events of his life may have an interest for others, but he alone is directly concerned in them. He is born alone. He dies alone. Between one being and another, there is a gulf, a discontinuity . . . But I cannot refer to this gulf which separates us without feeling that this is not the whole truth of the matter.* The whole truth of the matter.

Sarah arrives, walks towards me. She is almost twenty now. Her voice is changing, sharpening, the loose slang of New York giving way to a new articulation, a new vocabulary. She kisses me, and brushes on past, to Orr, lying peacefully with his eyes closed, as yet unaware. I wait just a little longer, for his inevitable awakening.

Acknowledgements

Many thanks to Tim Millen, Gail McConnell, Jude Sharvin, Jill Olson, Glenn Jordan, Paul Speirs and Amy Knight, Elliot Ross, Pete Rollins, Ben Behzadafshar; and especially Susan Davey, who always believed.

Also to Ursula Doyle and Ailah Ahmed at Fleet, for patience and encouragement and sharp editing; Denise Shannon; Lauren Wein and the team at Houghton Mifflin Harcourt; and my agent Nicola Barr at The Bent Agency, who made mountains out of molehills, and to whom I am endlessly grateful.

Credits

Pablo Neruda, *One Hundred Love Sonnets: Cien Sonetos De Amor*, University of Texas Press, 2014 (Sonnet LVII)

John Caputo, *How to Read Kierkegaard*, Granta Books, 2007

Jacques Lacan, *Seminar VII: The Ethics of Psychoanalysis*, Routledge, 2007

Samuel Beckett, 'Cascando' from *Collected Poems of Samuel Beckett*, Faber & Faber, 2013

Georges Bataille, *Erotism: Death and Sensuality*, City Lights Books, 1986

Samuel Beckett, *Watt*, Faber & Faber, 2009

Samuel Beckett, 'Malone Dies' from *The Unnameable*, Grove Press/Atlantic Monthly Press, 2009

Jean Vanier, *Becoming Human*, Darton, Longman & Todd Ltd, 1999

Søren Kierkegaard, *Fear and Trembling*, Penguin Classics, 1985

Samuel Beckett, 'Letter to Axel Kaun' from *The Letters of Samuel Beckett: Volume 1, 1929-1940*, edited by Martha Dow Fehsenfeld and Lois More Overbeck, Cambridge University Press, 2009